International Book Award Winner
(Young Adult Fiction)

Eric Hoffer Award Honorable Mention
Nashville Book Festival Runner-up

"[A] delightful and gentle fantasy is told in first person by Jaxon Mackenzie, a 12-year-old girl with autism....Mary Calhoun Brown has given us an unusual path in getting to the story of autism. Young teenagers, their teachers and parents will be happy to have this one in their library."~Dr. Ruth C. Sullivan, former President of the Autism Society of America

"[A] sweet, uplifting fantasy... The intertwining themes that run through this story are as powerful as they are subtle. Attitudes toward differences (whether racial or developmental) surface, as does the value and importance of true friendship.*There Are No Words* has a great deal to say! Its message is hopeful and timeless." ~Diane Twachtman Cullen, Ph.D., CCC-SLP, *Autism Spectrum Quarterly*

"Your love of the characters shines through... Great job!" ~Sara Hunter, award-winning author of *The Unbreakable Code*, a Smithsonian Notable Book for Children

"*There Are No Words* is lovely. A fascinating entry in the world of autism through an endearing character going back into time to rescue her grandfather's best friend. In addition to being a great piece of writing, this book is for anyone wanting to learn more about autism from an 'inside' view. *There Are No Words* has my highest recommendation." ~Stephen Shore, author of *Understanding Autism for Dummies; Beyond the Wall: Personal Experiences with Autism and Asperger Syndrome; Ask and Tell: Self-Advocacy and Disclosure for People on the Autism Spectrum*

"A wonderful story of a twelve-year-old girl, Jaxon, being raised by her grandparents. The author writes with so much detail that you will find yourself cheering for Jaxon during her adventure and learning so much from her even though she is unable to speak. This book will be adored by young teens, teachers and parents." ~Reviewed by Lara Blanchard, M.A., BCBA, MAAP Services for Autism and Asperger Syndrome

"A dream-like adventure that reads like poetry while challenging stereotypes." ~Feathered Quill Book Reviews

"I give high praise to the author, Mary Calhoun Brown, for being able to help me understand and experience life in a way that an autistic child might. How many times do we overlook or simplify what autism is simply because we do not understand it or have never experienced its effects in our lives? How frustrating it must be to be that child. To have to wonder about life every day and yet never have any answers to your questions. Jaxon was truly blessed to live with someone as intuitive as her grandparents. *There Are No Words* is a charming and likeable story, and I recommend it to readers of all ages." ~Charline Ratcliff, Rebecca's Reads

"Mary brings her characters to life with an infinite attention to detail and infuses them with depth, humor and selflessness. *There Are No Words* propelled me into a time and place in which even children were faced with the realities of racism and war." ~Mike Grady, CEO of the Autism Services Center, Huntington, WV

"This was a great historical adventure story. Mary Calhoun Brown made the characters interesting and children will enjoy this story and it will help them to understand others who might be different than they are." ~ Review TheBook.com Member Janice Hidey

"Your book is a beautiful, genuine story about love and friendship."
~Heidi Cortner Boiesen, IBBY Documentation Centre of Books for
Disabled Young People, Norway

"Jaxon's world is engaging from page one, the author's simple, quiet
style lending itself well to such a gentle, thoughtful read. ... Love and
tolerance are certainly abundant, but unlike most teen books in this niche
it is balanced with sorrow, anger and prejudice in real-life doses, which
rescues it from sentimentality and gives it a whole new dimension of
excellence. ... A heartwarming tale of trials and triumph, judgment and
acceptance; one that challenged my beliefs and brightened my day."
Maggie Desmond-O'Brien for KIDS Reader Views

"The most terrifying future is a future you cannot change. *There Are No
Words* tells the story of a mute girl who finds herself with a voice, but
sent back decades ago. With the knowledge of a train wreck that will kill
one of her grandfather's friends, Jaxon MacKenzie finds herself in a time
before said accident. But a twelve-year-old girl can't do much to stop a
government train...can she? *There Are No Words* is a charming story of
determination and friendship, highly recommended." ~Midwest Book
Review

"I am *loving* your book! I love the figurative language.... you are a
Reading Teacher's dream come true!" ~Melanie Alley, M.A., Fifth
Grade Teacher, Columbus City Schools, Columbus, OH

"This book is one that makes the reader look at lives of others [in] a
whole different light while it adds a bit of whimsy and 'what if' to round
it out. I suggest this book for readers of all ages, and especially those
who want a more positive book about autism than they have previously
read. It is a 'keeper' in every sense of the word." ~ReviewTheBook.com
Member Susan Pettrone

There Are No Words

MARY CALHOUN BROWN

all my best,

Mary Calhoun Brown

Lucky Press, LLC
Athens, Ohio USA

Published by: Lucky Press, LLC, PO Box 754, Athens, OH 45701-0754
Email: books@luckypress.com   SAN: 850-9697
Visit the publisher's website at www.LuckyPress.com
Visit the author's website at www.MaryCalhounBrown.com
Purchase order fax: 614-413-2820   email: sales@luckypress.com

PRINTED IN THE UNITED STATES OF AMERICA

Cataloging in Publication Data

Brown, Mary Calhoun.

There are no words / Mary Calhoun Brown. -- Athens, Ohio : Lucky
Press, c2010.

p. ; cm.

ISBN: 13-digit, cloth: 978-0-9776300-7-3; 10-digit, cloth: 0-
9776300-7-2; 13-digit, pbk: 978-0-9776300-2-8; 10-digit, pbk:
0-9776300-2-1
Audience: ages 9 and up.
Summary: A story of determination and friendship. Jaxon
MacKenzie, a mute girl with autism, is suddenly sent back decades in
time. She knows that a train wreck which happened on July 9, 1918
will kill one of her grandfather's friends, but a twelve-year-old girl can't
do much to stop a government train...can she?

1. Autistic children--Juvenile fiction. 2. Railroad accidents--
Tennessee--Nashville--1918--Juvenile fiction. 3. World War,
1914-1918--Tennessee--Juvenile fiction. 4. Friendship--Juvenile fiction.
5. [Autism--Fiction. 6. Railroad accidents--Fiction. 7. World War, 1914-
1918--Tennessee--Fiction. 8. Friendship--Fiction.] I. Title.

PZ7.B81653 T44 2010   2009937593
[Fic]--dc22   1002

In memory of my grandparents.

For the one who adored me
For the one who showed me strength
For the one who held my hand
And for the one who inspired me.

I miss you every day.

The deadliest train wreck in U.S. history occurred on July 9, 1918, when two crowded trains collided head-on at Dutchman's Curve. The impact caused passenger cars to derail into surrounding cornfields, and fires broke out throughout the wreckage. Over 100 died, including many African-American workers journeying to work at the munitions plant near Old Hickory.

—Dutchman's Curve historical marker

There Are No Words is a work of fiction and descriptions of events and characters are fictitious creations of the author's imagination. The Nashville-bound train accident of July 9, 1918 was a true historical event. History reveals that a man named Oliver Pack did die that day. Also, a Robert Corbitt was about to be embalmed when he moved. He lost his leg after the accident, but continued to work for the railroad and then survived another train wreck, later in life, by jumping from the train.

Acknowledgments

Thanks to my earliest readers, Cam Brown and William Brown. Huge thanks to my "that" exterminator, Allyson Ey. Thanks and a lifetime supply of Hot Tamales to Dr. Diana C. Bell for refusing the red pens I bought her. Thanks to Dewey and Harrison for believing in me. Special thanks to Louetta Hale Jimison, who deciphered my very first works of fiction, and kept one or two. Thanks to Pete Calhoun and Herman Allison for permission to use the painting for the book cover. Special thanks also to Janice Phelps Williams who took a chance on me and made my work better.

Biggest thanks of all to God for blessing me with stories to tell.

Credits: Front cover photo taken by Eric Michaud and licensed by iStockphoto. Painting on back cover by Herman Allison. Collection of Peter R. Calhoun and used with permission. Author's photograph by Janet Wise Mc-Cormick. "God Doesn't Love Me Any Less" © by Robert W. Kurkela and used with permission. (www.kidzpoetz.com). Appendix list, in part, provided by Tony Attwood and used with permission (www.tonyattwood.com.au).

God Doesn't Love Me Any Less

From the first day that I was born
There surrounded me a mighty storm
Not of lightning, thunder, hail or rain
But how people see me not the same.

On the outside I may appear quite slow
But I think some things they'll never know
Try as I may to share my mind
The words I want to say I can't find.

When I do talk I look away
People's eyes I tend to evade
It's not that I'm ignoring them
I listen yet my senses don't blend.

A single sound becomes my focus
And although I can feel your closeness
The bark of a dog fills my brain now
To listen and talk . . . I don't know how.

I touch but things feel different to me
Lotion to you may be glass to me
So if I seem to act somewhat strange
It's just that lotion causes me pain.

I learn through pictures more so than you
That's how I learned the sky is blue
This storm that surrounds me makes me smile
For I know that my life is worthwhile.

Though I'm not quite like all the rest
God doesn't love me any less.

Robert Kurkela
www.kidzpoetz.com

Sarah Hale and Dewey MacKenzie

Chapter One

If you looked at me from above, like a fly looking down . . . or peeking in through the wide parlor window from outside, I probably resemble any typical twelve-year-old girl. I like to lie with my back on the floor and my knees bent over the edge of the sofa. Grandma doesn't care if I put my feet on the old couch. She doesn't even mind if I leave my shoes on in the house. This is how I know she loves me.

As I rest here, staring at nothing, my fingers push against the dark olive green carpet. I like the way the individual carpet loops feel when I push against them. Each fiber is well worn and pliant, folding back against itself, singular yet connected to all the others. Most people only see carpet as carpet. Or they don't notice it at all.

When I lie like this, I like to stare at the oil painting that hangs over the sofa. My uncle painted it a long time ago. He's some kind of an artist, I guess. I don't see him much. He lives in Florida. I always imagine him and my aunt standing beside an orange tree. I don't even know if they have an orange tree, but it makes a good picture in my mind.

Anyway, a tree stands right of center in the painting. The regal trunk is a mixture of browns and grays, and, when you really stare at it, you begin to notice the white and black he used to shade and cast light. It *really* looks like a tree. I've never been good at painting or drawing. My trees always look like a kid drew a tree on a piece of white paper. But Uncle Charlie's tree is alive on the wall. When the furnace kicks off and the old house is perfectly quiet, you can almost hear the leaves rustling. I'm sure he used ochre and burnt sienna to paint the landscape of leaves. I like thinking of the names of colors. When I grow up, I'd like to be the person who names colors. I will sit at a big desk, lean back in my chair with my feet propped up on the top and my eyes closed, and I will imagine the most beautiful sounding colors.

When the first drops of rain fall outside the parlor window, it feels uncomfortable. I'm not sure anyone else can feel it. The water screams the minute it hits the ground, not a sound you can hear, but a vibration so high pitched, I want to cover my ears or hum. It's a lonely sound. It makes me want to cry, but I don't cry anymore, so I just wait it out. Before long, the steady rhythm of the rain shushes away the painful whimper of each drop as it collides with the earth. After a while, the wet pavement welcomes each drop. Sometimes I kneel by the window and watch as the water flows together. It rolls off the brick cobblestone street and along the cement curb. Sometimes when the drops melt together like that, they will find a leaf or a rock in their path, and watching the water bump over the leaf with a tiny splash that no one can hear makes me smile to myself. It's a secret.

I know lots of secrets. I am a very good listener.

*E*very day Grandpa and I take a walk. We have done this every day I have lived here with my grandparents, which has been such a very long time that I don't miss my own home at all any more. I belong here. I think I have an old soul.

My grandpa is very old. He was ancient when I was born, and he hasn't changed one bit. Most of the hair on top of his head has rubbed off, but he keeps some around the sides to show he can grow some if he wants to. Grandpa has the eyes of a giant. He told me once that the eyes are the windows of the soul, and I think he would win a Biggest Soul contest. His glasses are very thick, and they magnify his eyes. When he takes off his glasses, there are red marks on each side of his enormous nose and his wiry eyebrows are more noticeable. He looks like a completely different person without his glasses.

Grandpa's hands are dry and papery, and they are crooked when they bend. He holds my hand while we walk along the tree-lined avenues of our hometown. Sometimes we go over to the local college and watch the squirrels dance from tree to tree. The limbs wave goodbye to the squirrel when it jumps to another tree. I think I can hear a sad shushing sound as the tree realizes the squirrel has gone. I have to be careful when we walk because the tree roots have moved the sidewalk into jagged edges. Clumps of grass grow between the cracks. There is no steady rhythm to walking with odd angles jutting up, trying to trip us. Grandpa never stumbles. I am so thankful for that. If he fell, I'm not sure I would know what to do or how to get back to Grandma for help.

Grandpa talks to me all the time even though I can't talk back to him. He tells me of the olden days and of a friend named Oliver. Most of what I know of the world I learned from our walks. Grandpa knows the Indian name for squirrel; and once, when he was a young man, he took a pretty young lady sledding down past the old mill and crashed into a tree. Both Grandpa and the lady were just fine, but when my grandmother heard from the neighbors he had been courting another girl, she decided right then and there that she'd marry him. Grandma and Grandpa ran off the following week. Grandpa says he "knew just what he was doing." I believe him.

Grandpa tells me my mother is coming to visit tomorrow. I'm glad he tells me these things, even if I wish I didn't know. Mother wears navy blue suits with stiff, white starched collars that look as though they would rather break than bend. She always wears stockings that hide the freckles sprinkled across her legs. Her shoes are pointy in the front and high in the back. The heel digs into the dark green carpet, making a painful dent and some-times a snagging sound. They clomp on the hardwood floor in the entry way, and the clomping sound takes over the house as she gets closer to me.

My mother talks to my grandparents as if I weren't in the room. She doesn't always smile at me warmly the way Grandma and Grandpa do. I think she would rather be at the office.

Mother used to be softer before cancer took my father's life. I remember being very young, curled up in her lap. Her auburn hair was longer and soft, like feathers, to touch. She always smelled of Ivory soap and vanilla. She read *Green Eggs and Ham* to me over and over again. Sometimes she would skip words, but I always knew it. She didn't know I could read, even then. That's another secret.

I think I've always been able to read.

*G*randpa has a bookshelf next to the big feather bed where he and Grandma sleep. I sneak up there from time to time, careful not to leave knee marks in the overstuffed down comforter. The goose down pricks through the fabric and feels like tiny bee stings on my knees. I could go around the bed, and sometimes I do, but I'm always in such a hurry to choose a book and slip out undetected. I usually bound up and over the bed. The pages of Grandpa's books smell sweet and warm, like particles of dust dancing in the sunlight of early fall.

Today I have secreted away *The Lives of Illustrious Men,* by Plutarch. I have no idea what treasures it will hold. The cover is a chocolate brown with a Greek figure pressed into an oval in the center of the leather, and grapes and grapevines all around. None of it is in color. I like to imagine what colors the designer had in mind. The back is without decoration of any kind, and interestingly, when I close my eyes and run my hands over the front and back of the book at the same time, my fingers cannot detect where the indentions are. Both sides feel exactly the same.

I peek inside the tattered green cover of *The Canterbury Tales* one last time and run my finger across the faded pencil mark. It reads:

To DM from OP

I wonder who this book originally belonged to, then I place it exactly where it had been before. I read it through eight times, some stories more. I just love the wife of Bath. I'd like to meet her.

The problem with most books is that when I read them, all the adventures in the book happen to me right then. But the authors almost always write about everything in the past. Sometimes the authors will go on and on, describing a hill or a sunset, and I can't help thinking it wasn't worth remembering. If they would just tell what's happening when it's happening, then there would be no need to remember.

I smooth my grandparents' bed and tiptoe past the creaky part in the floor and into my room. I think this was my aunt's room before she married the artist and moved to Florida. The light through the two floor-to-ceiling bay windows has an amber glow that gives me the impression the room is scented with creamsicles.

There is a story about every piece of furniture in this old house. They call my room the cherry room, and the other spare room is the walnut room. I learned that the antiques in these rooms were made from trees that fell on my great grandparents' farm. The furniture in *my* room came from a cherry tree that was struck by lightning. As it turns out, Grandma's mother sent the tree to the mill to be cut into boards, and wrote to Eleanor Roosevelt, herself, to get plans to turn the wood into furniture. I never figured out why they had to get the plans from Eleanor Roosevelt, but I'm glad they did. My bedroom furniture has to be the most beautiful furniture ever made.

I can't remember the story about the walnut tree, how it fell, or how it came to be made into a bed, a dresser, and a night stand. I'm sure it is a fabulous story, full of people who lived lives that I'll never know about.

As I slip the *The Lives of Illustrious Men* under my pillow, I see the faded edge of a newspaper clipping sticking out of the top. Curious, I open the book and slide the fragile strip of print into my outstretched palm. The paper has turned brown, and its edges are soft.

When I carefully unfold it, the creases give way and the paper splits into four parts. Broken.

As I place the disintegrating pieces on the bed, I can make out the headline:

121 Persons Are Killed and 57 Injured in Train Collision
Death and Destruction Wrought When Crash on NC&StL RY Occurs.

Down the page is a list of the dead and injured. I close my eyes, but I still see the list burning white against the black of my eyelids. I hear a distant humming. Then I realize it's me. I rock myself back and forth to stop the humming. The image of the mangled train echoes in my mind as I feel the panic of the injured. Searing heat rushes through my core. Why would anyone keep a memento of such an awful event?

Once the humming stops I carefully fold up the news article, replace it in the old book, slip out of my room, and bound down the steps two at a time until I am four steps from the bottom of the staircase. I love the deep, resounding music of my feet as they hit the old wood. My favorite feeling, though, is flying through the air — so I jump. For the split second that I'm in the air, I feel complete happiness.

The bitter scent of Grandma canning pole beans in the pressure cooker hits me the second I land, and I know I will spend the afternoon on the wide wicker porch swing to avoid the stinging smell of the beans. Every image I have of Grandma is in the kitchen, standing on the fake brick linoleum with her back to me. Everywhere I am boney, she is rounded. Even her elbows and knees are soft. She often whistles, but never a recognizable tune. She smells of pie crust and oatmeal, and her hands are the most lovely hands I have ever seen. She wears a diamond ring that she never removes. She worries it with her thumb when she isn't paying attention. I'm sure Grandpa gave it to her when they were sweethearts.

Our old house sits on a corner. On one side, the streets are made of smooth cobbled Depression-era bricks. In front of the house there are two huge trees that block most of the paved avenue. From my spot on the swing, I can see a large white home cattycornered from us with four columns out front. I'm sure this once used to be a grand home. There are Greek letters on the side of the house, and bouncy young women wearing pastel colors and hugging textbooks to the front of their sweaters often come in and out of the house, giggling to each other like little mice.

The swing is a very special place for me. Grandpa often sits with me, and he sings songs. He scolds me for not wearing shoes out here. The porch is a blue-gray, like a dolphin, and it looks very clean. Grandma sweeps it every day. Somehow, though, after I have been on the porch, even for just a minute, the bottoms of my feet are always black with dirt. This is a mystery to me. My feet are black even now, and I've just walked a few steps on the dolphin gray floorboards.

The porch swing is a deep, forest green. It has been painted over so many times, the bends in the wicker are barely there. When I run my finger over the back of the swing with my eyes closed, the smooth bumps are rhythmic. And when I gently rock the swing, it sings "geeop, wee oooh, geeop, wee oooh, geeop, wee oooh." Nothing could be better, except maybe looking at the painting in the parlor.

Swinging is like flying through the air without the trouble of landing, so I'm happy to spend my day this way. When his errands are complete and the big white car is gently returned to its place over the greasy spot in the garage, Grandpa slides into the swing next to me. He pats my knee with his withered hand, and takes out the newspaper. He reads the headlines aloud to me, and my grunt indicates I want to hear him read the whole story. We work the crossword puzzle, and Grandpa fills in the wrong answer, probably on purpose. I point to his mistake. His warm embrace and gentle eyes show me he understands.

By nightfall Grandma has aired out the house, and I snuggle under an afghan she crocheted and poke my toes out through the holes between the stitches.

My dear grandfather.

Chapter Two

On this particular day, my mother arrives just after breakfast, banging the screen door behind her, clomping past the familiar face of the antique grandfather clock and its swaying pendulum, toward the parlor where I lie on the floor with my feet in the seat of the old sofa. I can smell the acrid scent of her perfume before I see her. Her scent burns way back in my nose, almost in my throat. I have to swallow hard to make it go away.

I can feel her eyes on my feet, dirty already from my time on the porch this morning. I curl my toes to try to hide them, but it is too late. She turns to Grandpa, slaps an opened envelope on the side table and begins.

"What the hell is this?" she spits.

I hear the familiar noises of my grandmother in the kitchen stop as Grandpa gathers his thoughts and his patience in a prolonged silence.

"Well?" my mother asks.

"Looks like a letter to me," my grandfather replies.

"I'll tell you what it is, Mr. MacKenzie. It's a letter from the group home I spent months researching. The director says you have refused to send pertinent information about *my* daughter that is needed for the initial evaluation as to the feasibility of her living at their facility."

Her words are sharp, like the sidewalks outside — jutting and angry, waiting for a stumble.

Grandfather calmly responds, "I didn't feel the need to reply to Mr. Bruce's request, Catherine. Jaxon is doing just fine here with us."

"Fine? Fine! How can you possibly think she's doing fine? She is twelve years old and has never spoken a single word. Not *one* word. She lives in her own little world here with the two of you."

"Jaxon is happy and healthy, and we love having her here," Grandpa states in that matter-of-fact way he has when he is emphasizing a truth.

"First of all, I am not questioning her physical health. Secondly, with all due respect, the two of you are old. What happens when you are dead and gone? Tell me. What happens when you are unable to provide what you seem to intuitively know she needs?"

This last part my mother says with regret and guilt mixed in with her anger. I know she is disappointed. She is unable to understand me.

"For God's sake, Mr. MacKenzie! Jaxon is autistic. How do you know the care you and Mrs. MacKenzie give her is what she needs? We need to think of what's best for Jaxon." Her words feel like shards of glass piercing my eardrum, and her tone continues to rise until it feels as though the words would strangle her.

As I watch her eyebrows scrunch up and her face turn red, I consciously breathe slowly, but I can feel the humming start, and the rocking is never far behind.

My grandmother comes into the parlor, wiping her wet hands on a dishtowel, "Calm down, dear." She says these words to me, but I hear my mother take a deep breath. Grandma has always had a calming affect on those with their tempers flaring. She is an active listener, and even when I am sure she will respond impulsively, she always says something that diffuses the other person's anger. I want to ask her how she does it, but of course, I can't.

My grandfather never takes his huge eyes from my mother. When he speaks, his voice is calm and sure. I feel Grandma standing near me, the heat from her hand is near my shoulder, but not touching. My mother is staring at me, and as I look up at her, then past her, I notice the children in the oil painting move.

I have stared at that oil painting every day for as long as I can remember, and this is the first time I've ever seen movement there. It is the slightest motion.

The children are painted holding hands as they dance away from the tree, and away from me. But just this moment, I see the young girl's golden hair move as though by her forward motion. It's glorious the way the sun glints in her hair. The boy's hand starts to move, then freezes.

I can't believe my eyes. I move closer to the painting to watch the pair of children more attentively, but I do not detect even the hint of additional motion. Maybe I was imagining it all along.

My mother's argument continues to spin around me, like a tornado of words and hurt, although my humming blocks it out so I can't tell exactly what words are spoken. Grandpa answers back to every harsh word. His voice is my protection, like a heated blanket on a snowy day. My grandmother's responses slowly ratchet my mother's voice level back down.

Grandma stands next to me, her housedress brushes against me. I can see the tiny stitches where she darned her knee-high stockings. I can see the scuff on her sensible-heeled shoes. Her soft hand hovers above my shoulder in a warm blessing. When I am ready, I reach up and touch her hand. *Ahhh.* The electricity of touch. I can only take it in little spurts. But when her hand and my hand melt together, I feel the humming fade, and I watch my mother stomp back out the way she came in.

Today on our walk, Grandpa tells me another story about good ol' Oliver. You see, Oliver and my grandfather grew up together near the tiny town of Bartlett, Tennessee. Oliver's mother, a black woman named Sophie, worked for my great grandmother around the house: hanging out laundry on the line, harvesting and preserving the crops, tending to the animals, and such. Oliver and Grandpa became fast friends. They spent every single day together on the farm, working hard. And on Saturdays Grandpa and Oliver liked to roll up their britches and catch tadpoles in the creek while their toes squished in the Tennessee mud. In the fall when Grandpa had to go off to the old Courthouse School, Oliver worked odd jobs to try to help his mother earn enough to get by.

In today's story, Oliver was waiting outside of the school for the students to be let out so he and Grandpa could walk home together, as usual. Oliver had recently been asked to help out Mrs. Miller, a well-to-do lady who had recently donated seven acres to the school board for a brand new school. There was much for Oliver to do in digging a road for access to the new building site, and he was proud to talk about his day of work with my grandfather.

Oliver couldn't wait to tell Grandpa the news. One of the white men on the job had overheard a city official down on old Raleigh-Somerville Road talking about a new road project. Grandpa's father was always complaining about the state of the roads and the many repairs needed on his wagon wheels. My great grandfather was worried one of his plow horses would go lame in one of the pits along the road. They had even stopped going into town during the rainy season.

As the story goes, in an indication of the community spirit of the town of Bartlett, all male citizens between the ages of eighteen and forty-five were required to spend eight days a year building and repairing the roads. Grandpa says he and Oliver just knew they would be able to help, even though they were still barely thirteen.

So a couple of weeks later, Oliver and Grandpa trudged down past Cedar Hall on Broadway Road and the Nicholas Gotten house on Court Street to City Hall to register for road work. Of course Oliver couldn't go inside the stately brick building, being black and all, but Grandpa signed them both up, and that spring they spent a sweaty, dusty week together repairing the potholed road going past the Methodist church.

Grandpa smiles when he talks about Oliver. His eyes crinkle at the sides and the corners of his smile turn all the way up. There is something sad about his Oliver smile, though. I wish I had the words to ask him what happened to Oliver Pack. I wonder what stories old Oliver could tell about Grandpa.

When we return from our walk today, there is the distinct essence of cherry pie in the air. We breathe it in all the way down Elm Street, and we know Grandma has been busy this morning. We also know there will be warm cherry pie with our fried chicken for lunch.

With our bellies full, Grandpa and I sit down, as is our custom, to watch the noon news. I keep one eye on the television and the other eye on Grandpa. He sits in his rocking chair with the maroon seat cover, wearing the same grey pants and burgundy cardigan he seems to wear every day but Sunday. His saddle brown wing-tipped shoes tap the floor boards as he rocks and watches television.

First his head tilts forward slightly. That's how I know he is falling asleep. Then his mouth drops open and his head falls back against the cushioned rocking chair. That's when the cacophony of snoring begins. Twelve fifteen every day. I turn down the television while the newsman drones on about sports scores and the weather.

I tiptoe around Grandpa and leap up the stairs by twos to my room. The afternoon sun streams in and catches one of the crystals in the miniature chandelier. A beam of light explodes through the crystal and paints the wall with its miracle. I settle myself on the floor between the bed and the window, in the midst of the rainbow, and take out the hidden book. The broken bits of newspaper have been my bookmark these past days as I drink in the lives of the men on the page. Today I fold out the article to read it through for the first time. The vibrant colors have given me courage to separate myself from the tragedy. I begin to read the faded words of the *Nashville Tennessean*.

Washington, July 9.— The Railroad Administration announced tonight that George L. Loyall, assistant to the regional director for the South, has been ordered to Nashville to investigate the wreck on the N., C. & St. L. Railway. Mr.

Loyall is especially charged, the administration said, with fixing individual responsibility for the wreck, if that is possible.

Because somebody blundered, at least 121 persons were killed and fifty-seven injured shortly after 7 o'clock on Tuesday morning, when Nashville, Chattanooga & St. Louis Railway passenger trains No. 1 from Memphis and No. 4 from Nashville crashed head-on together just around the sharp, steep-graded curve at Dutchman's Bend, about five miles from the city near the Harding road.

Both engines reared and fell on either side of the track, unrecognizable masses of twisted iron and steel, while the fearful impact of the blow drove the express car of the north-bound train through the flimsy wooden coaches loaded with human freight, telescoped the smoking car in front and piling high in air the two cars behind it, both packed to the aisles with negroes en route to the powder plant and some 150 other regular passengers.

Just where lies the blame, it is impossible now to say. Officials of the road are silent. But one of three things is reasonably sure— that the engineer of No. 4 was given wrong instructions, ran by his signal or overlooked the schedule on which he was supposed to run. That he knew the Memphis train to be a little late, leads to the conjecture that he was attempting to reach the switch at Harding Station, a short distance beyond the scene of the wreck, before the inbound train arrived at that point.

The article goes on, but my eyes are drawn to the list of the dead. Staring at me from the center of the list is a name I think I recognize . . . Oliver Pack. The realization comes over me like a bolt of lightning, and I place the broken pieces of newsprint back in the book, hoping I am mistaken. But when I peek back inside, Oliver's name is still there. "Oliver Pack, colored."

This picture shows our home. The bedroom atop the porch is the "Walnut Room." The bay windows can be seen on the left. My bedroom, the "Cherry Room," was on the second floor. Our parlor with the painting was just below.

Chapter Three

We live in the city, and so our backyard is not the wide, open backyard of my imagination, complete with a field of wildflowers, a simple rocky stream with a maple tree standing guard. But we do have a white picket fence, and my grandfather has given his little plot of land charm beyond words.

The back porch is uncovered and unadorned. It simply overlooks the lush green grass and the small, efficient gardens. There are exactly sixteen steps from the porch to the lawn, and grandmother rarely employs them. She would rather stew about in the kitchen, making her usual sounds and creating the delicious smells that send Grandpa and me back up for mealtimes with our mouths watering.

At the foot of the stairs is a large window that opens from the outside. I am not allowed to play in there, as the space is filled with glass canning jars and the only way to get in there is to crawl through the window. I can't imagine how all that glass got down there in the first place. I've only seen my grandmother ease her oversized self down there once, and I worried about her all the while. She is just not as nimble as she used to be, evidently.

At the corner of the house and the fence is a crazy looking forsythia bush. Every spring it reminds me of a boy I once saw, his messy yellow hair sticking out in every direction. Just down from the forsythia is a locked gate; its hinges rusted shut long ago. Across the lawn is the tiny vegetable garden where we grow our sweet corn, green beans, and juicy red tomatoes.

Straight back from the house is the white-painted brick of the garage my grandfather built himself using the simple geometry he learned in secondary school. Between the white wall and the manicured lawn stand my grandfather's pride and joy, his roses.

Of course we grow red roses, for love and respect. My favorites are the deep pink for gratitude and appreciation, and the light pink for admiration and sympathy. Grandpa likes the yellow for sociability, friendship and joy; and my grandmother likes the red and yellow mixed that represent gaiety and joviality. The way I remember the meaning of the red and yellow mixed is I think of it laughing at the other roses for being only one color. The most prized rose we grow is the "Peace" rose, a pale yellow to cream hybrid, which was smuggled into the United States from France around 1945. My grandparents say it reminds them of all those brave souls who gave the ultimate gift for our freedom. I think it's pretty.

My grandfather feeds and waters and prunes. My job is to pull weeds. Today as I reach deep into the black soil with my trowel to pry a dandelion out by its detestable roots, I practice the words over in my mind. What would I say if I asked Grandpa about what happened to Oliver

Pack. I move my lips in the shape of an "O." I end up not saying anything at all.

*I*t has been three hours, and I am still awake. Being awake by yourself in a big room in the middle of the night is just about the loneliest feeling in the whole world. Even the bugs outside have stopped their racket and gone to bed. The water in the bud vase next to me is a container of moonlight with a pale pink rose rising out. I can hear the clock ticking downstairs in the foyer. It sounds lonely, like drips of water from the faucet down the hall. As my mind wanders, I think of the rust stain in the sink from all the constant dripping. There are also some seashell shaped soaps in there that I am not allowed to use. They match the blue and white seashells on the wallpaper. I have no idea why we have soaps that cannot be used.

I slip my legs out from under the cool sheets and test the creakiness of the floors with my big toe. The night air is chilly, so I slip on a pair of jeans slung on the back of a chair. Gently I make my way past my grandparents' room to the stairs. Usually I would be afraid to go downstairs by myself in the middle of the night, but tonight I feel brave. I feel my heart thumping in my chest. I don't know what to do when I get downstairs, I just know it is where I am going.

Downstairs I feel the blackness of night around me. The furniture I know so well looks mysterious and unfamiliar. The blue-white light of a street lamp peeks through the window in the parlor, and brightens the spot on the floor where I like to lay to look at Uncle Charlie's painting. I find my usual spot and curl up to watch the colors. It is just at this moment that I notice it is night in the painting, too. The cornflower blue of Uncle Charlie's sky has been replaced with the deepest violet. The little boy and little girl who so often dance away from me must have gone to bed with the rest of the world because I cannot see them at all.

Then I see the shoes. They are regular old brown leather shoes propped up against Uncle Charlie's beautiful tree. I begin to wonder if I'm imagining the shoes, as they have never been there before, I can assure you. Before I know it, I am doing something that Grandma told me never to do. I am touching Uncle Charlie's painting. The dried paint is smooth in some places and bumpy in others. I love the way the texture feels against the pads of my fingertips.

Guiltily, I look over my shoulder to make sure I'm not being watched. There is no chance of being found by my grandfather. I can still hear his sonorous snores from all the way down here. And if my grandmother comes down the steps, her heft on the squeaky floorboards will alert me well in advance.

I know I feel eyes on me, though, and at this same moment, I hear a soft giggle and a whisper, "Come with us. We've been waiting for you." And as I turn around to look again at the painting, I see her. The girl from the painting. She is standing right next to the tree, smiling at me with a mischievous grin.

As I reach out my hand to the painting, the girl also reaches out to me. Our hands grasp somewhere between here and there. Within seconds, I am swept away.

The first sensation I experience is the rushing of wind against my skin. I cannot decide if I am floating or standing still or flying. I feel weightless, anchored only by the girl's hand holding fast to mine.

The wind moves around me, but it produces no noise. I notice a complete absence of sound. The comforting tick of the hall clock is gone. The familiar creaks of the old house have been absorbed in silence.

I realize my eyes are closed. I open them. Swirling around me in a sea of color are images from the painting, brushstrokes, blobs of something surreal. I see the artist's pallet; I am part of it, merging with the riot of pigment around me.

I notice my breath now in regular intervals. Even though I should be scared, I feel calm. I look through time into the eyes of the girl in front of me.

The MacKenzie's farm house and Ida, the mare, harnessed for work.

Chapter Four

We stood for what seemed like the longest time, her hand in mine, staring. I had always experienced a kind of electricity when touched, but this time no shock coursed through my body. It was as though I were holding my own hand. She smiled at me, this girl from the painting, and I thought we would stand like that together for the rest of eternity.

The chill of the summer night was around us, and though I was wearing a long-sleeved t-shirt, I felt the goose bumps rise on my arms as I shivered. The girl wore a heavy wool navy coat over a lemon chiffon colored dress with a white Peter Pan collar. There was a hastily tied bow at her collar, and I looked down to see that she had on baggy, worn men's pants under her dainty dress, and thick clunky boots that clearly did not belong to her. Her smile made her quite pretty as it lit up the rest of her features, average as they were. There was a dimple in her cheek that was barely there. From her angles I could tell she was just a wisp of a girl, and the heaviest thing about her was probably a thick tangle of golden, curly hair. She was like no one I had ever seen before.

"You must be cold," she said. "Take my coat." And before I could utter a sound, she whipped the heavy coat around my shoulders and motioned to the old leather shoes leaning next to the tree trunk. The laces had been tied together many times as a means of repair. "I brought you some shoes. I'm Sarah, by the way." And she offered her hand. It stuck out there in the darkness, waiting patiently.

She looked at me expectantly. She was waiting for a reply. I moved to shake her hand quite as though I did this kind of thing all the time. I moved my lips as I had done this afternoon to practice the way it felt to speak. Then, a croaky voice said, "Sarah." And it took me a minute to realize I had spoken my first word.

"Sarah," I said again as a tear trickled down my cheek.

I have no idea how she knew I was mute, but Sarah was clearly as excited as I was to hear the sound of my voice, and she threw her arms around me with a squeal, and I knew that at that moment we were sisters. I had been so lonely in my world on the other side of the painting, but now I had a companion, a friend. The joy was all encompassing.

"I'm Jaxon," I managed to say, the cobwebs still audible in my voice.

"Nice to meet you," she said.

"I . . . I . . . I'm not from around here," was all I could say, but my mind raced with all the words I wanted to say and the questions I needed to ask.

"I know," she said. "We've been watching you from the trees."

"We?" I asked.

"Yes," she continued. "Dewey and me."

My confused look asked the question for me, so Sarah said, "Dewey is my . . . my good friend. We play in the woods here as often as we can."

I noticed her stammer as she attempted to describe the relationship between herself and the boy she holds hands with in the painting. One eyebrow arched higher than the other.

I'd always assumed Uncle Charlie had painted a brother and sister.

I slid my arms down into the sleeves of the great coat and plopped down among the fallen leaves to put on the shoes that were meant for my bare feet. The sweet fragrance of the damp leaves on the forest floor mixed with a hint of wood smoke from a fire surrounded me. When I finished tying the battered laces, Sarah said, "Ready?" And at my nod, she said, "Let's go."

We tramped along a worn path through the woods, pushing our way past stray branches and jumping over fallen logs. A tree frog croaked his funny little tune. The ground was spongy beneath our feet. A rotten log rested dark in the shadows between peeks of moonlight shining in the full canopy of leaves above us.

Suddenly it occurred to me to ask where we were going. I wasn't used to conversation, back-and-forth talking, so the line between thinking my thoughts and speaking aloud was one I was reluctant to cross.

"Where are we going?" I managed.

"We've got to tell Dewey you are here. He wanted to come with me, but his mare was foaling, so he had to stay behind to help his papa. We weren't sure you'd come tonight, but I had a feeling," she said. "Ollie, too, and I've learned to trust *his* feelings."

And, without another thought, we traversed the speckled moonlit path through the forest on our way to see Dewey; the snapping of twigs beneath our feet and the shushing of branches as we passed were the only sounds now. Before long there was a clearing ahead and I could make out a small, white, clapboard church, complete with the requisite steeple. Beyond the little church was a dirt path leading up an incline, past a weathered wooden shed. This is the direction Sarah lead me. Once we turned past the shed, Sarah started to run.

"Come on," she called.

I ran behind her, sailing across the yard. I could have been flying except for the clunking shoes on my feet. I welcomed the chilled night air into my lungs as I ran on and on.

Sarah stopped at the edge of another clearing, and ahead of us I could see a house, painted the same white as the church, so it glowed in the moonlight. It was a traditional southern house with a covered porch and upper balcony with intricately carved spindles and floor-to-ceiling windows. Each of the upstairs rooms had a door with a screen that opened out to the balcony. There was an empty swing on the covered porch below.

Sarah panted lightly as I caught up with her, and we walked together the last twenty-five yards to the house. She marched up the steps to the main door and knocked hard. I heard footsteps approach the door, and then the homeliest woman I've ever seen greeted us. She was squat in stature and quite round in every sense of the word. Her hair was black with tiny whisps of gray and parted abruptly in the center. She had lines around her eyes that told me she was older, but the color of her eyes was clear, crystals of blue, cerulean, set off by a shock of black eyelashes any cosmetics company would pay big bucks for back on the other side of the painting. Something about her face seemed to be Cherokee; the arched eye or the narrow distinct nose, I couldn't tell which. She was dressed modestly in a simple green house-dress with a faded apron tied around her girth. She smelled like bread dough.

She opened the door and regarded me with mistrust, but when her eyes found Sarah's face, her own erupted in warmth and love.

"Good evening, Mrs. MacKenzie," Sarah began. Even with my limited knowledge of Sarah, I knew she was making the greatest effort at politeness for Dewey's mother. She stood stick straight, smiling, with her feet together and her hands clasped prettily in front of her.

"He's still out at the barn with the others, dear," said Mrs. MacKenzie, anticipating Sara's question before it was asked. Then Mrs. MacKenzie's eyes lit upon Sarah's pants and boots. "Are you wearing John's britches again?" At the hint of Sarah's dimple, Mrs. MacKenzie knew the answer. "Does your mother know?"

This time Sarah's blush was visible even in the darkness. "You won't tell, will you, Mrs. MacKenzie? How is a girl to help with foaling if she has to be all wrapped up in her skirts?"

Dewey's mother gave a knowing nod and motioned us toward the barn. We started to turn, then heard her say, "Next time, Sarah, dear, you should introduce me to your friend."

Sarah froze in place, grimacing at her mistake.

"I'm Jaxon," I said. Mrs. MacKenzie's eyes smiled at me and at Sarah, and we trotted down the front stoop and across the yard.

"Hmmm . . . Jackson." I heard her muse as she disappeared back into the house, wiping her work-worn hands on her apron.

An old photograph of Dewey (on the left) and Teddy with their grandparents.

Chapter Five

Approaching the barn with Sarah, I realized I was in a time and place unlike anything I had experienced before. The barn was dimly lit, as all barns seem to be. The smell of sweet hay greeted us as we rounded the weathered grey barn doors. I don't know what I was expecting. Perhaps a flurry of activity. Men in action. Someone calling out orders. Human intervention during the mare's time of need. The barn was silent.

There were three young men in the barn with their father. Two were balanced upon the wooden enclosure of the pregnant mare's stall. A third was on the floor with his back against a bale of hay and his ankles crossed, toes tapping. Three stalls were conspicuously empty, and with distant whinnying, I deduced the occupants were let into the enclosure for this horse to have some quiet while she gave birth.

The boys' father gave off the essence of a gentleman farmer. He leaned against the stall with one elbow crooked over the edge. Everything about him was well worn. His boots had seen many winters and many repairs, but they were solid. His shirt was worn at the edges and,

I could tell, soft to the touch. I guessed this was his favorite work shirt. His eyes were deep set with dark eyebrows seemingly more prominent with the positioning of his hat. It was set back on his head, as though he had momentarily tipped it back to wipe his forehead with a handkerchief and forgotten to move it back into place. The most striking feature of this kindly man was an unruly salt-and-pepper handlebar moustache that began on one side of his chin, traveled up his face, across his upper lip, and made its way back down the other side of his chin. It was a monument to moustaches everywhere. I could tell it was a source of pride for Mr. MacKenzie, for this was surely who I was seeing. I imagined him as a young man, courting Mrs. MacKenzie when she was a girl and much thinner; combing his moustache before taking her to church on Sunday.

The two boys on the stall looked as though they could be twins, although one was slightly larger and, upon closer inspection, I could tell the larger boy had the longer nose of his mother, while the smaller boy had the wide, handsome nose of his father. I knew one of these boys was the one I had been spying in Uncle Charlie's painting, but for the life of me, I could not tell you which boy was Dewey. Of course, in the painting, Dewey had always been dancing away from me through the woods with the girl I now know as Sarah.

The young man reclining in the hay was much older, nearly a head taller, and was heavier boned, heavier jawed and just all around heavier. He could never dance through the woods. He would rather chop them down. I could see it in his countenance.

The men tipped their hats to Sarah and me, and I knew this was not a time for introductions, but miracles. The mare's hind quarters glistened with sweat, and she kept looking back at her rump. Her breathing was even, and occasionally she would move her nose back to sniff and then she made a sort of snorting sound. She seemed restless and spent some time moving from her side, where she was lying, to a standing position and back. Pieces of straw stuck to her chestnut coat.

"It's just about time," Mr. MacKenzie whispered in our direction. And as I looked at him, I noticed a movement off to the side, a shifting. Then a bright smile gleamed out of the darkness, and my eyes adjusted until I saw the blackest young man I had ever seen in my life. It's no wonder I didn't see him initially. He wore a dark shirt and denim overalls that seemed to blend with the saddles and horse blankets along the back wall. His hair was cut so short it looked more like a shadow than anything, and his ears stuck straight out on either side of his head with considerable mirth. The bottomless dimples on either side of his mouth only deepened as his smile stretched further up his rounded cheeks. Laughter played around his eyes.

I smiled at him. There was really nothing else I could do. The smile started right in the middle of my chest and worked its way up until my cheeks stretched tight across my face and my eyes were so squinty I could barely see.

"Dew, Oliver, grab those rags and a bucket of fresh water," commanded Mr. MacKenzie with calm authority. The taller of the look-alike boys and the black boy fell into step next to each other.

About that time the mare heaved herself up on her white-tipped hooves and expelled a great stream of water. I had, of course, never seen an animal (or anything else) give birth, so it wasn't until later that Sarah and Dewey explained that this was the fluid surrounding and protecting the foal when inside its mother.

The mare lay back down on her side, and I watched as her belly began to heave regularly, and within minutes a sack the size of my arm protruded from the rear of the horse. With more contracting and heaving, the mare managed to push out the head of the foal, which was of course still inside the sack surrounding it. I could make out the twitching and moving of the ends of the sack, and I realized there were two tiny legs in the front part of the sack, and they were indeed moving. Warmth like a thousand lights pricked through my chest and my eyes began to water. This was a miracle. I was witnessing a miracle.

Every eye in the barn was concentrated on the scene in front of us. No words were necessary. A final push from somewhere inside the mare and the work was complete. A foal was born.

"Good job, Ida," Mr. MacKenzie crooned at the mare. She looked at him. Then she admired her foal. She sniffed and snorted and made vocalizations to her baby. She licked him dry and let him know he was hers, then she lay back down to rest after her hard work.

The foal had no intention of resting. He wanted . . . no . . . needed to explore this new world. Where his mother was all chestnut with white on her nose and the ends of her legs and hooves, the foal was a swirl of chestnut and white. Two hooves were white and two were chestnut. His face was the perfect blend of color, and his eyes were endless pools of innocence. He tried his front legs. They wobbled. He tried again, attempting to use the weight of his body to push himself on to his legs. They wobbled again. For what seemed like ages the tiny foal struggled to stand. I began to worry that perhaps there was something wrong with his hind legs. His mother watched him as she rested. She snorted something to him. He tried again and again. Finally, the little foal thrust his weight to his front legs and caught his wobbling back legs behind him and he stood.

I didn't realize I had been holding my breath, but at that moment, all of us in the barn let out a collective sigh. Tears streaked down my face, which burned red with the shame of crying, but then I looked at Sarah, and she, too, was crying. I imagined I saw a glint in the eyes of all four of the boys, even the tough one.

"James MacKenzie," said Dewey's father, offering his hand to me.

"Jaxon," I offered.

"Miss Jaxon, it is a pleasure to make your acquaintance," he said.

Then, one of the look alike boys stepped next to me and interjected, "I'm Dewey," and he took my hand into his eager hand and pumped my arm up and down with such enthusiasm that we began our acquaintance in laughter.

"You look really familiar," he said.

"Dewey?" Sarah asked. "Look closely at Jaxon. Don't you recognize her?"

Dewey studied my face. Oliver eyed me cautiously from a few steps away.

"The girl from the trees." I couldn't tell if it was a statement or a question, but I could tell Dewey had somehow recognized me.

Within seconds I was sandwiched between Sarah and Dewey, each with one arm around my shoulder.

In one swift motion, Dewey climbed the rickety ladder to the loft, sat cross-legged, looking down at us. "C'mon up," he said.

Dewey's smaller brother started up until Dewey pushed him off with a practiced twist of the ladder. "Not this time, Teddy."

I had lost all timidity. On this side of the painting I had decided I could be someone new. I belonged. After all, I had only been here for a couple of hours, and I already had made my first two friends ever, excepting (of course) Grandma and Grandpa. I scattered up to the loft and landed in the soft hay. Next to me there were two black kittens pawing at the hay as if it were alive. They tumbled over each other as only kittens can do. One of them had a tiny white spot between its ears.

"What are you waiting for?" I asked in Sarah's direction. The words hung in the air. I loved the sound of my voice, deeper than Sarah's but feminine.

Sarah climbed up and plopped down next to me. "Hold my ankles," she said. I grabbed one, and Dewey grabbed the other as Sarah leaned over the edge of the loft. Her torso hung over the edge of the loft, and I was glad she had thought to put on the pants under her skirt. With her hair falling, a golden waterfall in the lamplight, Sarah called out for Oliver.

"You coming?" she asked.

Oliver leaped up, catching the edge of the loft in both hands. He arched his back and swung his legs back and forth until his body's momentum allowed him to pull himself up with his strong arms. The way his shirt laid across his chest and shoulders hinted of a muscular build, and his skin was the perfect shade of dark chocolate.

"Oliver, this is Jaxon," Sarah began. "Jaxon, I'd like you to meet my *dear friend* Oliver Pack."

The painting that hangs over my grandparents' sofa.

Chapter Six

The name rang through my ears. *Oliver Pack. Oliver Pack. Oliver Pack.* I felt dizzy and unconnected to everything around me, but when I searched the faces of Sarah, Dewey and Oliver, I felt a calmness surround me, a feeling of home. I took a deep breath. Could this be my grandfather's Oliver?

Sarah's introduction had emphasized the words good friend. There was a subtext to her words that I determined to discover as my acquaintance with Sarah grew.

"It's nice to meet you," I said and Oliver nodded in reply.

"My grandfather used to tell me stories about a friend he once knew named 'Oliver.' I've always liked that name. They were friends a long time ago."

Oliver grinned in a glorious way. "I'd sure like to hear those stories sometime, Miss Jaxon."

"It seems Grandpa's Oliver was quite a character."

"Well, this Oliver Pack is as real as they come," he said patting his chest with his hand. "There's no books that can hold me. No characters here." His dimples were cavernous.

We all laughed.

An expectant silence followed, and I noticed Sarah and Dewey sneaking glances at each other. They were two parts of a whole. Anyone could see it.

"What?" I asked.

Dewey answered, "So, Jaxon, how did you get here?"

It was a simple question to which I had no answer.

"I snuck downstairs late at night, and I reached out to touch the painting, and I touched Sarah's hand instead."

I knew my answer was incomplete and made little sense.

Sarah stepped in to fill in her side of the story, "I saw Jaxon reaching out of the trees, and I grabbed her hand, and it was akin to pulling her out of a bush."

"Sarah and I have been watching you from the woods for weeks," said Dewey.

"But how could you see me in the woods? I watched you from the painting in my grandparents' parlor."

Sarah began, "We noticed the leaves as the wind blew. They would shift and rearrange into a girl's face. At first I didn't say anything to Dewey. I thought it was my imagination. All I could see at first was your face. When I mentioned to Dewey that I thought I could see a girl's face in the leaves, he said he had imagined it, too."

"There's a clearing out past the Miller's place, where Sarah, Oliver and I have always visited," Dewey continued. "When we were little, we would sneak up there and pretend it was a secret clubhouse. Sarah's mother doesn't take too kindly to Sarah playing with Oliver, so we have to be really careful."

Oliver lowered his eyes. I could tell he was sad about having to hide his friendship with Sarah. Yet their friendship was as natural as Dewey and Sarah's was.

My grandfather's friend Oliver was black also, and I remember Grandpa telling me people didn't like white and black folks to interact socially. I couldn't understand a world in which the color of a person's skin determined whether they could enter a building or be someone's friend. I was being raised differently. Grandpa had read newspaper articles to me about racial unrest, but in my simplistic little world, I was oblivious to the history and scope of this kind of hatred.

I just kept thinking, "If only people on my side of the painting could be as accepting of me as these two white children are of Oliver."

Sarah said, "So one day not long ago, we saw great sadness in your face. Your expression was pained. That was the day you saw me turn away. We had been so careful to go unnoticed, but that day—"

"I remember," I interrupted. "It was the day my mother came to visit. She was arguing with my grandparents. She wants me to go away to a special boarding school for autistic kids, and my dad's parents are fighting her. They want to keep me."

"That night Oliver had a strange dream," Sarah continued. "He often has dreams warning of the future. His great-mammy was that way, too. Anyway, you tell her, Oliver."

He nodded. "In my dream, there you was. You wasn't leaves, but a real young lady who needed us to pull you through. And later on in the dream I saw you pullin' me out of the dark, and I know you was comin' to us for a reason. Now all we need to do is figure it out."

How could I tell my side of the story?

"I have no idea *why* I'm here," I began. "I live in a different world than this. Where I come from, I can think, but I can't speak. It's called autism. People there think I'm stupid, or they think I'm deaf. I don't know how many times a well-intentioned person has spoken down to me or screamed in my face in the hope of being heard. My sense of touch is tenfold what it is here. I can feel touch before the person makes contact with my skin, and when skin meets skin the noise in my ears is almost unbearable. I hum to make it go away. Sometimes I rock back and forth to comfort myself. I like to think I rock as a way to remember how it used to be with my mother, who started pulling away from me when my father died. But when I was little, she used to rock me in our big white wicker rocking chair every night and whisper songs into my hair."

Dewey said, "If you can't talk, how do people know what you need?"

"My grandparents just seem to know instinctively what to do and when. Their days are pretty much regular. I like the predictability. Plus, they talk to me. Other people pretend as though I'm invisible or they treat me as though I were contagious."

Sarah was thoughtful as she bent her head to one side, "So why do you think you can talk here with us?"

"I'm not sure. I've been making more of an effort to speak at home. I move my mouth and will the words to fall out, but so far nothing has happened."

Oliver sailed a piece of hay through the air, and it landed in Sarah's golden tangles. "I think too much talkin' is wasted breath. It's like when we was working on the roadways a couple a months past. Why, we fixed up that road without two words between us. We just didn't need no words. And now, good ol' Ida'll be safe when she heads on into town. Maybe that's like you, Jaxon. You're savin' your words up. That's alright by me."

Oliver's intelligent eyes shone in the dim light. *Saving my words.* What could be so important to say that I would have to wait all this time to say it? I wondered if I would ever utter a word in my world or if I would ever return there again.

"Now that I'm here, where will I stay, and how will I get back home? Maybe I'm just dreaming."

"You're not dreamin.' Trust me. There's no explanation for this," said Dewey.

"You can stay with me," Sarah offered. Dewey shot her an incredulous look. "I'll work it out," she mouthed in Dewey's direction.

The next hour was spent deriving unique and sometimes potentially painful ideas for sending me home when I was ready to go. As I giggled and shrieked with Oliver, Dewey, and Sarah, a sneaking thought crept into my head. I was having so much fun in the hayloft, I wasn't sure whether going home was something I ever wanted to do. I felt real and alive in a way I had never felt before.

As the night wore on, I was struck by the bright and thoughtful way Oliver spoke and the honesty of his every word. Oliver seemed part child and part preacher. Except for his ears, his was perhaps the handsomest face I had ever seen. He seemed wise beyond his years, and I felt the poverty and oppression of his race in the sadness of his eyes. His only flaw, as far as I could tell, was a deep-rooted stubbornness that was expressed only when Dewey told Oliver what he should do. It wasn't that he resented Dewey. I could tell he wanted to figure life out for himself. That's just the way he was.

Similarly, Sarah's strong will defined her character. She lived in a world of aristocracy, at least as far as the town of Bartlett was concerned. Due to her mother and father's position as wealthy landowners in the town, Sarah's steps (and missteps) were closely monitored by the busybodies to fuel their jealous gossip about one of Bartlett's finest families. Frequent were the lectures she endured from her mother, all wrapped up in her silks, with regard to how a "young lady" should act. Sarah's rebellion was manifested in wandering the countryside and wearing her brother's britches and shoes under her freshly pressed pastel frocks. With her father's secret blessing, Sarah tramped through the woods, befriended one of the MacKenzie boys, and tolerated her mother's displeasure at regular intervals.

Sarah's father called her "Tot," and she was clearly the favorite among his children. He enjoyed arguing points of debate with his daughter and quietly wished she had been born a boy so her quick wit and strong will would not be dragged down by petticoats and good manners. Sarah's weakness for Dewey was clearly her greatest trial. She wasn't openly smitten, but her tender care for Dewey was evident, and she often berated him for incidences in which he could have been injured. Of course, he was just "being a boy," as they say, but she scolded him nonetheless.

Dewey was thoughtful and calm. Where Oliver was quick witted and charming, Dewey's words were filled with logic and straight talk. He was someone who stood up for those who had suffered injustice. His opinions, once formed, were solid. Dewey was accustomed to hard work, both on the farm and in the classroom. He educated himself outside of the classroom by reading philosophy and studying the Greeks. He loved poetry, but his attempts at creativity in that art were wasted. He was fiercely protective of Sarah, his mother, and his younger sister Elizabeth, who had lost a leg to polio. He was polite to those who were his "betters," and only seemed to bend to the strong will of his father, James, and to the stronger will of Sarah Hale.

Our night together in the loft seemed to last for days. I became practiced in my newfound ability to converse, and I was drawn in by the personalities of those around me. In the dim lamplight of the barn loft, and with the two kittens purring softly in my lap, I began to understand the preciousness of friendship.

Mr. and Mrs. Hale, Sarah's parents.

Chapter Seven

Yawns all around announced to us it was time for Sarah and me to leave the barn, and so we said our farewells to Dewey and Oliver and smiled at the strong foal prancing in the stall. We headed back toward the little whitewashed church. Quick as a whip, Sarah slipped behind a bush and shimmied out of the pants and mud-caked boots. From the shadows beneath the church, she emerged looking quite pretty wearing clean, dainty slippers and picking bits of hay out of her hair and dusting off her yellow dress.

"How did you do that so fast?" I asked.

"Years of practice," she laughed.

"Where did you put your things?"

"There's a hollow space between the ground and the floor of the church above. I keep my play clothes in there when I'm not wearing them, and I hide my good shoes there when I'm out and about. Mother scolded John about losing those pants, and he would tan my hide if he knew I took them.

"Now for the real test," she smiled at me slyly, arching one perfect eyebrow higher than the other. "We have to get you past my mother."

Moments later I stood in front of an impressive white brick home whose entrance was marked with a formidable stone fence and pointed wrought-iron gate. Sarah flipped the latch with one practiced motion, pushed open the gate and motioned for me to go ahead of her. The house was striking with its black shutters and lacy curtains in each window. An expansive porch spread around three sides of the house and the path up to the porch steps was paved with flagstones. A low, manicured hedge surrounded the porch, and I noticed carved stone urns flanking the entrance, each planted with a perfectly proportioned Alberta spruce. The delicate porch furniture looked as though each piece had been made of gingerbread.

Sarah grabbed my hand and brought me around to the side of the house where three simple steps lead up to a plain kitchen door. She hesitated.

"Jaxon, we're going to need a story of who you are and where you came from. My mother will insist on introductions, and you look, well, unpresentable. We can sneak through the kitchen to the back stair, and I'll find some appropriate clothing for you from Helen's room — that's my sister, of course."

"I could be a cousin . . . from somewhere."

Sarah snickered. "Yes. You're Dewey's cousin, visiting all the way from.... Bristol, Virginia. I think that's where his papa's people are from. And we hit it off at the foaling, and you've come to spend the night."

"But what if your mother talks to Dewey's parents?"

Disappointment washed over Sarah's face. "There's no chance of *that*," she replied.

Within ten minutes, my face had been scrubbed pink. I had been stuffed into unusual under-things then buttoned into a full-length wool skirt with a starched white high collared blouse with puffy sleeves and delicate lace around the neckline. I was impressed with my reflection in the looking glass as Sarah and her sister Helen tamed my unruly hair into something quite nice.

Helen was nearly as tall as me, but delicate in every sense of the word. Her demeanor and manners were impeccable. She smelled faintly of lavender, and her motions were as graceful as they were filled with purpose. She was an obedient daughter, but delighted in Sarah's tendency toward mischief. Helen secretly wished she were more like Sarah, but seemed peacefully resigned to the fact that she simply could be no one other than herself. When I think of Helen, I think of her timid smile, downcast eyes and faintest blush. She apologized profusely with every stroke of the wide brush as my tangles crackled through it, even though my mess was none of her doing.

As the girls put their finishing touches on my appearance, the only problem was my shoes. Helen and Sarah both had delicate, small feet, and my feet had been compared to barges on more than one occasion. There was nothing to do but wear the worn out brown shoes I'd had on since that first moment in the forest, and try to conceal them beneath the floor-length wool skirt. I practiced scrunching down slightly as I walked, and Sarah burst out laughing. Helen tried to suppress her giggles, but they bubbled out of her.

"Try to calm your countenance, dear," Helen suggested between fits of polite laughter.

"You're making a funny face," Sarah clarified.

"How's this?" I asked, making every effort to remove expression from my face without succumbing to the giddiness of the fellowship of friends.

Both girls agreed I was ready to meet their mother. I must say I was scared to death. I had to remember the story we had concocted, to scrunch my body and maintain a serene expression on my face. I could feel beads of sweat form on my upper lip. The wool skirt did a great job of hiding my shoes, but it was lousy at helping me keep my cool.

We tiptoed our way down the back stair. Once outside in the cool night air I carefully lifted the skirt to avoid the mud, and Sarah fell into a giggle fit. She imitated me to display what had caused her such mirth, and I couldn't help but snicker. What a pair we made!

As I climbed the steps to the porch, I practiced my slouch to suppressed titters from Sarah. A lazy tan-and-white beagle with chocolate brown, genial eyes was curled upon the welcome mat with his nose tucked beneath one of his velvety, freckled paws. He lazily stretched toward Sarah and rolled to reveal his belly.

Sarah patted his belly and rubbed his silky ears, and I did the same. She cooed at him, "I love you, Darcy. You're the best dog in the whole world." And I could tell she was right. His tail wagged madly, and I swear Darcy smiled at us.

The foyer of Sarah's house was breathtaking. Straight ahead to the left and right of us was a double staircase joining at the landing and proceeding to the second floor with a crimson runner and brass carpet rods. Helen stood with one hand on the banister, smiling down on us, an accomplice to our mischief. A distinctive crystal and alabaster chandelier hung hyalescent in the electric candlelight. The honeydew-colored walls were hand painted down to the black and white checkered tile floor with flowering botanical greenery and small, lifelike birds.

To the left a door was open, and I could see a pine-paneled library filled with dark, important-looking books and a fine Chinese rug. The cushions were of soft leather, and the room was punctuated with a substantial cherry desk. Bent over the desk, making notes in the lamplight, was an older gentleman in a three-piece suit, complete with pocket watch. He looked at us with kind eyes as he slid his watch from its pocket, and exaggerated his surprise at the news the watch imparted.

"Isn't it a bit late for a young lady to be coming home, Tot?" he asked in a deep baritone with a twinkle in his eye.

"The MacKenzie's mare was foaling, Papa," was Sarah's reply.

"There's no rushing it," he commented.

"No, sir," she said. "Papa, this is my friend, Miss Jaxon. She is a cousin of the MacKenzie's, and I'd like to invite her to stay the night with us."

Mr. Hale stood and made his way to me. He offered me his warm hand, and I shook it gratefully. His welcome felt like a hug, and I took a deep breath. "S'nice to meet you, Miss Jaxon," he smiled. He was a man of few words, but he put his heart into every one he used. I liked that.

"Thank you, sir," I said. "It's very nice to meet you, as well."

"You better take Miss Jaxon in to meet Mother, Sarah." He winked.

"Yes, sir."

We passed again through the foyer and through double French doors which announced the entrance to the Hale's parlor. My eye was instantly drawn to the uniquely carved fireplace and mantle. The mantle was painted white with intricate scallops, scrollwork, and a center carving of an urn. Flanking the fireplace itself was a creamy marble that made me think of warm vanilla pudding with caramel swirls. Mrs. Hale had a small fire in the grate, and she sat with her needlework basket next to her on an overstuffed yellow sofa. She didn't look up.

Sarah stood up straight. "Excuse me, Mother. I hope I'm not interrupting."

Mrs. Hale seemed to ignore her as she continued to pull long pieces of sky blue embroidery thread through the fabric and the embroidery frame, frowning.

We waited. I felt a trickle of sweat escape down the middle of my back.

"Sarah," she broke the silence without looking up. "Would you please ask your *guest* to wait in the foyer while I have a private word with you?"

"Yes, Mother," Sarah replied. I was already headed out to wait, scrunching down to hide my shoes as fear sent heat waves to my extremities. Sarah indicated a chair for me to sit in. "I'll be right back," she winked, mimicking her father. Then she closed the parlor doors behind her, and I saw her mother's piercing eyes for the first time as she regarded her daughter. Sarah stood solidly in front of her mother, ready to reply to each question asked of her.

Sarah the Brave, I thought as I noticed the worn brown tip of a shoe peeking out from beneath my hem. I tapped my foot in rhythm with the comforting tick of a massive grandfather clock. Its swinging brass pendulum entertained me as I waited and listened.

"First of all, young lady," her mother's voice chided clear and sharp through the closed doors, "where have you been keeping company so late into the evening?"

"I was at the MacKenzie's, Mother. I was—"

"Excuse me for interrupting," Mrs. Hale began without a hint of remorse. "And what, pray tell, were you doing over there so late at night, young lady?"

"The mare, Ma'am, the one I told you about, Ida? She was foaling—"

Her mother spoke more harshly this time, "Excuse me for interrupting, again, *dear*, but you really should not be spending your summer in a barn."

It was as though Mrs. Hale felt using a term of endcarment would make her rigid tone more loving or acceptable in some way. It only succeeded in making her sound more disingenuous.

Sarah continued, "And I couldn't tear myself away before the baby was born."

"And you have been there the entire time, in the company of Mr. and Mrs. MacKenzie, I presume?"

"Yes, Ma'am. Mr. MacKenzie stayed in the barn the whole time."

"And you were never left unsupervised while in the company of those . . . *children*?" Mrs. Hale asked, her steely eyes boring into Sarah's.

The vehemence in the way her mouth moved around the word "children" was pronounced, and I could see that Mrs. Hale, for all of her good breeding, obvious beauty and stiff poise, saved her kindnesses for those of her limited acquaintance rather than those in her immediate family and her neighborhood.

Sarah looked her mother right in the eye and lied, "No, Ma'am."

How Sarah managed to keep from becoming a puddle on the floor in response to Mrs. Hale's thinly veiled politeness, I will never know. Later, when I thought over their exchange, I realized Sarah must have developed strategies to deal with her mother's spite. Anger and disappointment lurked in Mrs. Hale just beneath the surface, and I could not figure out to what Mrs. Hale could attribute her obvious displeasure. She lived in a fine home with every comfort of the day. Her clothing was elegant and flattered her curvy figure. Her husband seemed to be a successful yet quiet man. Mrs. Hale had someone to cook, someone else to clean, and countless others to maintain the property and work the family garden.

"Well, I can't imagine how you managed to stay so clean, spending the evening in an old barn! Now, who is this *poor creature* you have brought home with you?"

Knowing that Mrs. Hale would be unlikely to strike up a conversation in town with Mrs. MacKenzie, Sarah used it to her advantage. "She is Mr. MacKenzie's niece, Miss Jaxon. She's visiting from...Bristol, Virginia, Ma'am. We met over at the MacKenzie's, and I thought it would be proper for me to invite her over."

"It would have been more proper, dear Sarah, to invite her over for lunch, but—"

"But Mother—" Sarah interrupted.

"Do allow me to finish my sentence, young lady," she insisted. "Since you have put your heart in front of your head, once again, dear girl, I will be introduced to Miss Jaxon, and she may stay."

Before long, although it seemed like a long time to me, Sarah opened one of the doors to admit me to the parlor and to greet her mother. Sarah had a triumphant look on her face.

Our introductions were brief, and Mrs. Hale was short with me, but the result was as we had hoped, and Sarah and I loped up the stairs to her room. I was relieved the interview was over and that I had a comfortable place to spend the night.

Chapter Eight

Even through my fatigue, I had trouble sleeping that night. As I stared at the ceiling I tried to piece everything together in my mind. The last time I had lain down, I had been on the other side of the painting in my own bed. Clearly I had fallen back in time through the painting. Two thoughts would not leave me alone.

The first was that the two Oliver Packs, my grandfather's Oliver and the Oliver I had met tonight, were one and the same. But my grandfather's Oliver was dead. He'd died in the famous train wreck from the brittle newspaper article.

The other was a secret I had kept from Sarah, Dewey, Oliver, and all the other kind folks I had met today. I didn't want to raise any questions that I couldn't answer, so I didn't tell anyone that my first name is Jaxon, but my last name, which no one bothered to ask, is MacKenzie . . . the same as Dewey's. So when Sarah introduced me as a relative of Dewey's, she didn't know it, but she was telling her mother the truth. The confusion for me was that Dewey in no way resembled my ancient, balding grandfather. I was determined to look around the next day to see if I could make sense of the puzzle in my head.

I awakened the next morning to the delicious smell of frying bacon and the sound of Sarah whistling tunelessly as she dressed. When she noticed me stir, Sarah tossed a worn pair of overalls at me.

"You'll need these today," she said with a hint of mischief. "Don't let my brother, John, see them."

My apparel for the day was not what one would expect for the middle of July, and I wondered how I would manage not to look ridiculous. Beneath the full length wool skirt and blouse borrowed from Helen the night before, I wore John's overalls and my own shirt. The bumps from the buckles were clearly visible, and the thick denim fabric caused Helen's skirt to fall short, exposing the clumsy, scuffed leather shoes.

I wondered aloud how I would pass her mother's scrutinizing gaze in daylight, no less, with such attire, but Sarah calmed my worries. Hurrying down the back stairs and grabbing a fist full of bacon and biscuits, we escaped a meeting with Mrs. Hale.

As we trudged down the lane, I was overcome by the blooming of the countryside around me. The near complete darkness of the country night, now behind me, had given way to a glorious morning filled with birdsong. The crisp night air surrendered to warmth as the sun inched its way higher in the sky. Each step we took startled crickets and katydids from their unseen repose. Yellow finches flitted from tree to thistle and back again. Whole fields of wildflowers, daisies, and black-eyed susans, strained sunward. The air, pure and clean, smelled of sweet honeysuckle and freshly cut hay.

Sarah barely seemed to notice nature's splendor as she chatted away in anticipation of seeing the foal and his mother in the field. I crawled with Sarah beneath the church and then carefully removed Helen's clothes, folded them, and placed them in the nook where the toes of Sarah's dainty shoes peeked out. In one practiced motion, Sarah pulled the pants on beneath her dress and slid each foot into her oversized, muddy boots.

We found Dewey and Oliver already hard at work. Without a word they each rhythmically added to the heaping pile of dung outside the barn. Teddy carried buckets of water from the pump and dumped each bucket with considerable splash into the large troughs for the animals. The farm was alive with MacKenzies, buzzing about like worker bees, completing their morning chores.

After our "good mornings" to the boys, Sarah said, "Let's find Mrs. MacKenzie and see if there's anything we can do."

I was happy to follow her. We found Mrs. MacKenzie next to the house pruning the dead heads from a trellis overflowing with the palest of pink roses. She was instructing a delicate, towheaded girl of nine to go inside to help with lunch, while one youngster of about five dug up weeds with a fallen stick and a toddler of no more than two hung from Mrs. MacKenzie's skirt.

Doling out instructions with practiced ease, Mrs. MacKenzie sent us to the garden to pick pole beans and dig up new potatoes. When our baskets were full, we sat on the old porch swing, pinching the ends carefully from each bean pod and pulling the waxy string down each side. By the time we had snapped all the beans and scrubbed the potatoes clean, our fingernails were packed with deep, rich, black soil. I loved it.

Lunch was served at a rough-hewn table beneath a sprawling chestnut tree. I found myself staring at Dewey, looking for a nugget of recognition. I was convinced that if I stared long enough I would remember an old tin type or photograph of a relative resembling him. His hands were powerful and strong, and he gestured with them as he spoke. His eyes were large and filled with kindness, and they had a spark of playfulness, especially when he regarded Sarah. The history of friendship with Dewey and Sarah was palpable, and anyone who spent more than a minute with those two could tell their future together was certain.

With my attention on Dewey, I didn't at first notice the pointed looks and gestures flying between Oliver and Sarah when Dewey wasn't looking. Clearly there was something Sarah felt Oliver should tell Dewey, and Oliver was dragging his feet. Dewey must have noticed it, too.

"Alright, you two. If you have something to say, then say it, for heaven's sake."

Oliver playfully pushed Sarah's shoulder back and frowned theatrically.

"Well, go ahead, tell him," she smiled.

"I'm takin' a job. Out o' town. There. I said it, and that's that."

"What? When did this happen? Why didn't you tell me?" Dewey's feelings were hurt. He worked side by side with Oliver every day, and Sarah had been the one Oliver confided in.

"I know you'd try n' stop me, but there is too many mouths for my mama to feed, an' mose of the men-folk in my family are off fighting."

Oliver kicked at the dirt with the toe of his boot and studied the dust as it settled back down.

"But where? What are you going to do?"

"My cousin, you know the one, mama's sister's boy, George Scott? Well, he's leavin' on the Number One train to Nashville tomorrow mornin' to go make powder in the DuPont plant up at Old Hickory. I'm goin' with him. We've never been on a train before, so we're real excited."

I know I heard Oliver say he was taking a train, and I understood what he said; but I didn't put the pieces together right away. I remember feeling a sense of dread or anxiety as Oliver spoke, and I realized that Oliver Pack would one day die aboard a train headed to Nashville. Still, I remained silent.

Dewey's face grew concerned. "But you know, Oliver, my mother will give your mother anything you need while your family is off fighting the war."

"Awwwl, Dew. I'm fourteen years old. It's time I be growin' up and workin' like a man. Charity's alright for children, but I gotta make my own way in this world."

"Where will you stay?" Dewey asked.

"George Scott's got a roomin' house all lined up. We be staying there mose the time. I'll be sleepin' on the floor, but I figure I'll be real tired and won't miss my feather mattress too much."

The boys volleyed questions and answers all through lunch, and then continued their conversation as they worked side by side in the stifling Tennessee heat.

Sarah and I found little activities to occupy our time and help Mrs. MacKenzie. But as the day wore on, I felt uneasy. I tried to dismiss it as a reaction to my new environment, but it felt more like foreboding. I could not shake the feeling no matter what I did. I rationalized it as unease about facing Mrs. Hale again.

We washed up the best we could using the pump in the front yard of the MacKenzie's house. No amount of scrubbing could remove the dirt beneath my fingernails. We stopped at the little church to change clothes, and headed for home.

Sneaking through the kitchen door, we wanted to avoid Mrs. Hale and have a chance to find out from Helen the disposition of her mother. We were stopped short upon entering to find Mr. Hale in the kitchen. He was caught off guard when we entered, and looked guiltily at us before breaking out in a grin.

"You've caught me," he said. He held a piece of baked ham smothered in a brown sugar sauce, which he quickly popped in his mouth. "I couldn't wait until dinner. You won't tell, will you, Tot?"

Sarah laughed. "Of course, not."

"Well, girls, hurry upstairs before she sees you and wants to know where you've been all day."

Sarah playfully saluted her father, and he returned the gesture. Lucky for us, we took our supper with Sarah's siblings in the kitchen that evening. Mrs. Hale, evidently, suffered from headaches and preferred to eat in silence with her husband when her head bothered her. I couldn't help feeling sorry for Mr. Hale.

That night Sarah and I decided to pack sandwiches for George Scott and Oliver to take on the train with them. As she sliced the ham paper thin with the sharpest knife I had ever seen, Sarah said, "I think we should surprise Oliver with the brown paper sacks on the train platform.

Then once Oliver and his cousin are safely onboard, we can wave goodbye as the train pulls out of the station."

I knew Sarah imagined herself pretending to be one of the many military wives waving farewell to her brave soldier with a white handkerchief. Sarah's only concern about our plan was being spotted by someone who might tell her parents she was talking to a couple of colored boys at the train station before dawn.

It was a very romantic vision Sarah had, but I knew we couldn't do it alone.

"We need to get to the train station," I said. "And the only person we know who will take us there is Dewey."

"Don't worry about Dewey's help. You can be assured he will be happy to oblige." Sarah grinned and batted her eyes. "We can slip over to enlist his help after we finish the sandwiches."

I was getting excited about our plan. "Plus," I said, "he could act as chaperone to prevent any troublesome whispers getting back to your mother and provide transportation in his father's wagon for George Scott and Oliver."

By the time our heads hit the pillow, our covert midnight journey was set.

An old photograph of Mrs. Hale and Sara's sister, Helen.

Chapter Nine

The heat from the day lingered into the night, making it hot and sticky with humidity. Sarah kicked off the coverlet immediately, and neither of us could stand to lie beneath the sheet, thin as it was. My pillow was perpetually too warm, and I spent a good portion of the night flipping it to the cool side. Sarah and I were careful not to touch or even come close, and throughout the evening I felt her move to check the time.

We were worried about sneaking out of her house at 1:30 in the morning or oversleeping and missing our adventure altogether. Once we left the house, we were sure to be back within an hour, and no one would notice we weren't still tucked snugly into bed, but the excitement of the trip to the train station and the nonstop thoughts running through our minds ensured that neither of us rested that night.

As we slowly latched the kitchen door behind us, the night air was comparatively crisp compared to the heat still lingering in Sarah's room. Dew clung to each blade of grass, and our shoes were soaked by the time we arrived at the MacKenzie's barn. A herd of deer stood inside the enclosure for the horses near the dark outline of the woods. They stood at attention with their white tails at the ready as they heard us approach the barn. All the stars came out to greet us in full force, brighter than I had ever seen them before. As I looked up I felt lost in a galaxy of tiny lights.

Oliver practically danced over to us. "I didn't sleep a wink," he called as he crossed the yard.

"Neither did we," I said.

"Where's Dewey?" Sarah asked, but before Oliver could answer, we heard Dewey harnessing the horse on the far side of the barn.

George Scott was silent. He was a tall, brooding looking young man. Probably eighteen years old. Serious. He was wearing clean overalls for his first day of work in the powder plant. I wondered how dirty they would be after he spent a day making gunpowder. When he walked, I could detect a pronounced limp, and I knew an injury had kept him out of the armed forces. Working the factory was his act of patriotism.

Oliver was in perfect contrast to stoic George Scott. He rambled on in a nonstop stream of consciousness. In fact, I was sure he did not have an unspoken thought that morning. He talked about the work and how much he would be paid. He thanked us profusely for coming out to send them off. He mused about the train and whether they would ride in a metal or wooden car. He remembered (out loud) the first time he saw Jaxon in the trees, and he mentioned offhandedly that George Scott had a dream that something horrible was going to happen.

Finally Dewey said, "Hey, Oliver. Why don't you keep it down before you wake up the whole farm?"

With that, the horses were harnessed, and we were off. The bumping and jarring of the wagon wheels against the ruts and hollows in the dirt road reminded me of my grandfather and the story of how he and Oliver Pack had signed up to fill in the potholes. I remembered the soft sadness in his eyes as he talked of his friend, and at that moment I was homesick for my grandparents.

A myriad of thoughts swirled about in my head. There I was bumping along under the stars, having an adventure with the only friends I'd ever known, talking as though I'd been talking all my life. Part of me felt as though there was something to miss about being trapped without language in a world spinning so fast around me that I spend most of my time just trying to adjust. The rest of me was nearly giddy with the exhilaration of (what felt like) escape from my life.

I felt a shadow of guilt. Had my grandparents noticed I was gone? Were they worried about me? I remembered the furrows in my grandmother's brow when she was troubled. My deepest hope was not to cause her a moment's concern. A sigh passed my lips, unheard by the others, and the feeling of loss passed. I was again drawn into the conversations around me.

The station was buzzing with activity, and I felt an unshakable notion that it was midday rather than the middle of the night. Gas lamps lit up the platform, and men were moving crates and luggage about in preparation for a train. There were dapper young uniformed soldiers standing about in camp green with caps under their arms, and unlike Sarah's thoughts of tear-streaked young ladies waving goodbye, there were mothers in house dresses with weary expressions holding tightly to their sons' arms with both hands. The presence of the military was keenly felt all around the station. To one side of the platform an area was roped off, and black men stood shoulder to shoulder, crowded together like cattle, awaiting the train.

The bubbling anticipation and enthusiastic mood surrounding our trip to the train station evaporated. Oliver was really leaving.

George Scott and Oliver watched the commotion on the platform with rapt attention, each gripping a burlap sack that no doubt contained their clothes and any other belongings they deemed necessary for their life in Nashville. Dewey was unnaturally sullen at the prospect of his best friend going off for an unspecified time and remained silent as we hopped down from the wagon.

The darkness around the station was made darker by the illuminated platform. George Scott's face reflected his thoughts, and suddenly I felt an overpowering sense of dread.

Sarah and I found a worn bench under one of the gas lamps and began unloading the sandwiches for Oliver and George Scott.

Oliver said, "I'm much obliged to your kindness, Sarah," and his sad eyes told me how much he would miss her.

He turned to me. "Miss Jaxon, I'm sorry to leave just as I was gettin' to know you. I know you'll take right good care of Sarah while I'm gone, and I'll be back before you know it."

"Oliver," I began, but a lump in my throat prevented me from saying how I felt. I wasn't sure if I would still be in Bartlett or on this side of the painting when Oliver returned from Nashville. All I knew at that moment was the pained feeling of anticipated loss.

In the meanwhile, Dewey pumped Oliver's hand and slapped his back in a tender gesture of friendship and love uncommon among young men.

"Are you ladies ready?" Dewey asked, clearly ready to hop back in that most uncomfortable wagon and drive us home.

"But we came to see them off," answered Sarah, and added hopefully. "Didn't we?"

"It's your hide," he said, referring to the obvious fact we were being most disobedient to Mrs. Hale and her expectations of young ladies.

"Just until the train pulls away, please, Dewey?" she pleaded, her eyes catching his for a moment longer than necessary.

"It's your hide," he repeated, bowing slightly.

George Scott and Oliver each tucked three sandwiches into the burlap sacks. George stood stiffly, but Oliver smiled his dimpled, perfect smile at Sarah and whispered, "I shoulda hugged you back at the wagon, Sarah. I can't do it here among all these white folks. You take care of ol' Dew for me, wontcha?" And he offered her his rough, black hand to shake.

Several disapproving eyes stared at Sarah's fair hand clasping Oliver's dark hand. "Thank you for comin' and for the sandwiches," he said to both of us.

"Yes, thank you," said George Scott in a quiet voice. He never made eye contact with us, and always looked at the ground.

"You're welcome," we replied as Oliver and George Scott made their way into the crush, roped off for their race. Sarah and I sat on the worn bench and watched the activity around us as Dewey paced back and forth on the platform.

"Are all these military men going on the train?" I asked to no one in particular.

Dewey replied, "The federal government has commandeered the railways during the war. They need to send supplies here and there, and they don't want anyone to know what is going where. They need the railways to transport troops and messages back and forth. My father says it's a mess, though."

"How so?" I asked.

"Anytime the federal government takes over something, everything that can go wrong, *will* go wrong."

I was instantly reminded of my grandfather and his family. Grandpa had instructed me on the Civil War and of the dangers inherent in a strong federal government. All the MacKenzie men had been states' rights proponents, and a dislike of large government pervaded each man to the core.

"Dad says the trains are running late; the schedules are all confused so regular trains aren't so regular anymore, and you just can't count on the mail service at all."

I glanced absently at the clock near the top of the station's roof and noticed Oliver's train was already ten minutes late. I was conscious of the spaciousness of the part of the platform where we now sat and the disparity between the levels of comfort offered to us versus the standing room only area where Oliver and George Scott stood crushed together. A rope ran across the platform from the station to a pole near the tracks with a sign reading "Coloreds," and by my guess eighty percent of the passengers stood behind this rope in a small area that probably encompassed just twenty percent of the platform. This made no sense to me. Why not just let everyone stand together on the platform?

Each passing minute made Dewey more restless. I could tell he was nervous about what would happen if Mrs. Hale discovered we were gone and realized Dewey had been instrumental in our escape. I could almost hear her haughty voice frequently interrupting Sarah as she tried to explain our absence from home.

Peeking through the sea of bodies, Oliver could sense Dewey's uneasiness, and motioned for us to go just as Locomotive Number 281 pulled into the station. It was thirty-five minutes late. The engine pulled two sleek sleeping cars of steel construction, one baggage car and six wooden coaches. The white passengers were loaded onto the sleepers, and we watched as Oliver mounted the steps into the wooden coaches with the other black passengers.

I glanced at Dewey for a brief second. He had a certain tilt of his head that was by now familiar. But on that morning, he was stooped just a bit under the weight of Oliver's leaving and his worries over Sarah and me. His eyes seemed to grow larger with sadness, and his eyebrows were furrowed as though he were deeply concerned.

That was the moment.

Suddenly the truth was clear. I was standing next to my grandfather. I had seen the same expression on his face thousands of times. The sadness in his eyes was the same as I had seen when he mentioned his Oliver Pack.

The platform seemed to become jelly under my feet, and my hands reached out on either side to steady myself. Each hand found its way to the shoulder of my friends, and I cried out, "Nooooooo."

It wasn't the voice of the confident young lady who had come into her own these past days. It was the strained voice of a girl who had never spoken before. It was my own voice. A voice from my side of the painting.

Sarah and Dewey both regarded me with shock, and Dewey attempted to lead me back to the wooden bench. I wrenched myself away from them and ran toward the train.

"Come back," breathed Sarah, but I could not stop myself as I bolted onto the train. Dewey was on my heels, but stopped at the threshold of the train.

In a moment of the purest clarity, I knew why I had been sent through the painting. My mind flashed back to the faded edge of a newspaper clipping. The soft edges of the brown paper appeared in my mind as though they were before me. The four pieces, broken and lying on my bed, when pieced together read, "121 Persons Are Killed and 57 Injured in Train Collision." My mind scrolls through the article and stops cold at the listing of the dead and the name of "Oliver Pack."

I remembered Oliver's dream. He said I needed to be pulled through the painting, and then later in his dream I pulled him out of the dark. I had not understood what it meant to pull him out of the dark, but now I was sure.

The pleading look of incredulity on Dewey's face as I stood in the metal doorway of the sleeper car shook me from my memory. I reached out and grabbed his hand and pulled him towards me. Sarah was not two steps behind him when the train began to slowly pull out from the station. She walked along side the train until she neared the end of the platform, grabbed the handle and jumped on the train.

Nashville Tennessean newspaper, 1918.

Chapter Ten

A nd so there we were. The three of us. On a doomed train without tickets. Barreling through the darkened Tennessee countryside. A horse and wagon tied up at the station awaiting our return, and no earthly soul knowing where we were.

Although his eyes showed alarm, Dewey's voice was calm. "What are you doing?" he asked as the train lurched, and we reached out for stability.

A kindly man in a blue train uniform bustled past and asked us to find our seats.

"Come with me," I whispered to Sarah and Dewey as I grasped Sarah's hand, and we made our way through the first sleeping car. My head was spinning. I searched for a place for the three of us to sit, but nearly every seat was filled. Toward the end of the car I noticed the entrance to a vestibule and to the right there was a nearly empty closet.

The three of us slipped into the closet without being noticed and seated ourselves on the floor, below a small window.

"Will you explain, now?" Dewey asked impatiently.

"We have to save Oliver," I said.

I wasn't sure how to explain my behavior, but I was absolutely certain I would stop the train.

"This train is going to wreck," I began, "and Oliver is going to die today unless we can stop it."

"So you jumped aboard?" Dewey asked.

"What else was I supposed to do?"

"Send a telegram?" he offered.

"And who would believe me?"

Sarah said, "How do you know this, Jaxon?"

"I read it in a newspaper article back on my side of the painting. This train runs head-on with another train. This is my purpose here with you."

"How did you come across this newspaper article?" Dewey asked.

"I found it in your book."

"My book?"

"*The Lives of Illustrious Men.*"

"Plutarch?"

"Dewey, I've got news for you. I'm your granddaughter. Jaxon MacKenzie."

Sarah and Dewey stared at me as though I had two heads.

"Unbelievable," he muttered, shaking his head, but I could tell he knew I was telling the truth. "When did you figure all this out?"

"On the platform as I stood next to you, your expression of sadness at watching Oliver go was the same as it always was back home when you would talk about Oliver Pack. You missed him so much."

"Why didn't you recognize me before?"

"Dew, you're an old man to me. You wear thick glasses. You almost never take them off, and you're bald and wrinkled."

"What about Sarah?"

"I can't say I recognize her, Dewey."

Dewey took a moment to process the information I had just provided him. Sarah's face was thoughtful. She somehow had accepted the outrageous information I had just given them and had made the decision to help.

"So what do we do?" Sarah asked.

"I say we go to the engineer and ask him to stop the train."

"Just like that?" Dewey asked.

"Why not?" was my reply. "If he stops the train, we save the lives of everyone onboard."

Dewey looked at Sarah in that way that he had, adoringly, protectively.

I peeked around the corner and found no one coming. Everyone on the train appeared to be settling in for the trip. The doors to the private rooms were shut, and beyond the narrow passageway, the passengers in coach were quiet. The three of us made our way past them.

A woman knitted silently next to her sleeping infant. A businessman snored quietly two seats away. A young soldier read a newspaper with the headline "French Advance Along Compiegne Road Northwest of Antheuil."

At the front of the car, I opened the sleek metal door and stepped outside the protected walls of the steel sleeper car. The rattle of the connectors and the clickety clack of the train wheels were inaudible from the roaring of the great engine now before us.

The gravel between each railroad tie was a blur as I

looked down to carefully step over the gap and onto the platform behind the engine.

A brusque man in a midnight blue uniform stood before us.

"You have no business up here," he said, pointing back in the direction he wished we would return.

Behind him in the brightly lit space were four men, all smoking cigars and clapping one man in particular on his back in congratulations.

"I need to speak to the engineer," I said.

"That is not possible, Miss," he replied.

"It is an emergency," I continued.

"There is no emergency you could present to me that would cause me to disturb Engineer William Floyd from his work this morning," he said curtly.

"We are on a collision course, sir," I pleaded.

"You children need to go back to your seats *now*," the man directed.

"But, sir," I interrupted.

"May I see your tickets, please?" he spoke over me.

Sarah tugged at my dress from behind.

"Let's go," Dewey said.

I stood woodenly for a moment. Hands on hips. Defiant for an instant, and then made my way back passed the dozing passengers and into the tiny coat room where our strategic planning would begin.

Dewey said, "Jaxon, we're going to have to jump from this train. I can't risk your life and Sarah's."

"I won't jump without Oliver," Sarah said. "Not before we've done all we can do."

Both Dewey and I regarded her; he in disbelief, and I in admiration.

"Sarah," he pleaded, "we can send a message to the engineer through someone. Let's go before the train picks up more speed. As it is, you are likely to end up with broken bones."

"I'll borrow some paper and write a note to the engineer," she said.

"Dewey and I will go back to the wooden cars and warn Oliver and George Scott," I said, knowing it would be easier for me to gain entrance to the colored cars with an escort.

"We stay together," Dewey commanded. Then he said, "Jaxon, do you know how much time we have to give our warnings and get off this train?"

None of us had a watch, and I couldn't trust my memory as to the specific times in the newspaper article. All I could remember was the train wrecked in the morning. By my estimation, we had been on the train for forty-five minutes, and I could remember that Oliver's train was thirty-five minutes late.

"I'm not sure when the wreck happens, sometime in the morning. This train was thirty-five minutes late coming into the station. What time was the train supposed to leave, Dewey?"

"Ten after three."

"So we left at 3:45, wouldn't you say?"

"S'bout right," Dewey replied.

"It must be nearing 4:30. The collision happens just outside of Nashville, so I think we have a little bit of time to try to stop this train, maybe an hour, to be on the safe side."

A man's voice from the corridor announced, "Tickets!"

The three of us froze in place and kept silent until he was well past our hiding place. The minutes felt like hours. A bead of sweat trickled down my back, and at once it occurred to me that I had endangered the lives of Dewey and Sarah by bringing them along with me.

"The two of you should jump," I whispered.

"And leave you behind?" Sarah asked. "No. Absolutely not."

"I've put your lives at risk. I should never have done that."

"We are all in this together, Jaxon," Dewey said calmly. "Now let's go."

I took a tentative step into the corridor and looked toward the engine. The ticket man was standing next to a passenger speaking in low tones just steps away. I looked back at Dewey and Sarah with wide eyes and pointed in the opposite direction. "This way," I mouthed.

We slipped through the doors leading to the second sleek sleeper car, stepped over the connectors to the platform on the car behind ours, and entered. The berths were in the center of this car with coach passengers before and after the sleeping compartments. Unlike the previous car, this one had plush red carpet and curtains draped back from each window. Doors were shut to three of the four sleeper suites, but the door to the fourth was open. Inside I saw a leather booth, complete with table and a small glass vase holding a cluster of daisies. A man and a woman sat facing each other, deep in conversation. Hinged above the booth was a Murphy-type bed that could fold neatly against the wall. The couple had piled pieces of luggage atop the bed, which created a canopy over their heads and framed their image into quite a pretty picture.

Caught staring, I passed by the couple and continued through the car. I looked at each passenger to determine if he or she were napping, hoping to find someone with something to write on. An older couple held each other's weathered hands. A well-dressed young man smoothed the felt of his hat and fingered the tiny spotted feather stuck in the band. A soldier sat bent over with his head in both of his hands.

At the rear of the car sat a young woman of not more than thirty, dressed smartly in ivory linen with a matching hat. Her hair was jet black and pulled back loosely with an aquamarine ribbon just exactly matching the color of her eyes. I remember having seen her in the crowd at the train station in Bartlett. Her cheeks were flushed pink from the heat inside the metal railway car. The object that drew my attention to this beautiful woman was the pale violet stationery embossed with her initials that she filled line by line with perfect script.

I hesitated as I passed her, and behind me I heard Sarah say into my ear, "I see it. Go on."

Sarah paused casually next to the lady, "Mrs. Dunn?"

When she looked up from below her hat to speak to Sarah, I could see she had been crying. "Oh, Sarah," she began as she reached for a handkerchief from her neat little pocket. "Forgive me," she said as she dabbed at her tear stained cheeks. "Please, sit with me."

Mrs. Dunn moved a bag from the seat next to her and patted the cushion. I later learned that Mrs. Dunn, the former Bessie Poague, was an acquaintance of Sarah's sister. Bessie had married a local Bartlett fellow named Henry Dunn nearly five years ago, and just last week she had received confirmation that Henry had been killed in the war. She was making her way back home to Nashville to her family just then.

Bessie Dunn and Sarah's conversation was halted by Mrs. Dunn's frequent need to dab at her eyes and gain her composure. Three times I saw her take a ring from her left hand and show it to Sarah, only to have Sarah nod sadly and give it back to Bessie. I thought she would *never* get the paper, but nonetheless, after what seemed like hours, Bessie handed the paper to Sarah, along with a pen. Sarah scratched her note on the paper quickly, and returned the pen to Bessie Dunn. A few minutes were spent in goodbyes before Sarah finally hugged the unfortunate bride and made her way back to us.

Sarah told us that Bessie was distraught beyond words and insisted on continuing to write letters to her beloved Henry even though she knew she would never see him again. The mournful woman had repeatedly shown Sarah her diamond wedding ring, saying between sobs that she wasn't sure she would have need of it anymore. She said that it just reminded her of Henry and the life they had planned but would never have. Sarah's replies were comforting to the woman, but her tears ran fresh as Sarah walked away.

As we walked toward the back of the train and the wooden cars, we looked for a sympathetic glance or a kind expression from one of the railroad men, hoping we could trust someone with the note in Sarah's hand, still hoping to stop the train.

Chapter Eleven

An employee of the Nashville, Chattanooga, and St. Louis Railway stood at the entrance to the six wooden cars holding Oliver pack and the others of his race. He flipped absently through a handful of papers, less a sentinel than a secretary, but another stumbling block for us to maneuver on our way to Oliver.

I could see through the small window on the door that the first car (and probably those thereafter) was loaded to capacity with workers like Oliver and George Scott. The heat in there must have been stifling.

"Excuse me, Sir," I mumbled, trying to pass by without being noticed.

"Sorry, Miss. These last cars are for coloreds only." His face was unusually long and one eye was off-kilter with the other behind his thick, square glasses. He made a habit of perpetually pushing his glasses up the bridge of his considerable nose.

"I need to speak to one of the men in there," I said.

He looked up from his paperwork and into my face for a long moment, considering. "Can you see him from here? Through the glass, I mean?"

"No. He boarded in Bartlett, and I'm not sure which car is his."

"You'd have to go all through the cars to find him, Miss. I'm afraid I just can't let a young lady like you walk through there. It's for your own safety, Miss."

"Do you have a passenger's log? There should be some record of who is assigned to which car," I said.

"They're loaded in like sardines, Miss. We've got no way of knowing where the man is."

I was conscious of the train barreling ahead.

I looked imploringly at Dewey. His expression was almost apologetic. Wasn't he going to offer to go back to look for his best friend? Then I saw the determined look on Sarah's face and Sarah's delicate hand in his. I knew she had a plan.

In her other hand, Sarah held the note she had scribbled on Bessie's stationery.

Time was not our friend, but Dewey drew the railway employee aside. He spoke to the man and introduced himself calmly, offering his hand. His name was Robert D. Corbitt, and he was a breakman on the train. Dewey explained that the passenger we needed to speak with was Oliver Pack. Mr. Corbitt still refused to allow Dewey to go back into the colored coaches with two young ladies.

After much discussion, Mr. Corbitt kindly offered to deliver Sarah's note to the engineer, and with Dewey's promise that he would not take the "misses" into the rear of the train, he headed for the front of the train.

A splash of warm red tones on the horizon told us dawn was approaching. I had a sick feeling in the pit of my stomach that we really needed to get off that train. Once

Mr. Corbitt was out of sight, I slipped into the door of the first wooden car and told Dewey and Sarah I would return with Oliver before Mr. Corbitt realized I was gone.

Both Dewey and Sarah protested, but I was already among the crush of brown faces and stale air. The heat, stench and noise in the railcar were overpowering, and I felt twinges of sensory overload.

Everything in me told me to get out of there, but I would not leave without Oliver. I pushed through the crowd yelling at the top of my lungs for Oliver. I couldn't be sure that even the men around me could hear me.

By the time I reached the back of the first of the six cars, either my whiteness or my femaleness had created enough of a distraction to allow my now-hoarse voice to be heard above the din. "Oliver Pack!" I shouted, but there was no answer.

The next three cars were the same, and by the time I reached the fifth of the six wooden coaches, my clothes clung to my skin with sweat and my voice was just a notch above a whisper at its loudest.

I felt despair every time I glimpsed part of a window and saw the sun slowly climbing in the east. By then I was crying. I had been gone from Dewey and Sarah for easily over an hour.

Every second brought us nearer to Nashville and the inevitable wreck. My mind expected the train to slow at any moment once the engineer received Sarah's warning note, but we barreled on.

A powerful hand grabbed hold of my wrist and wrenched me around. I saw the red, angry face of Mr. Robert D. Corbitt. He bellowed, "Come with me!" and I was dragged back the way I had come. A sea of bodies in overalls and work shirts parted for us as Mr. Corbitt tramped through the cars with me in tow.

The noise I had experienced before was all but gone, and the lonely sound of the train moving down the track sounded to me like the ticking of a clock.

When he had dragged me back to where Sarah and Dewey stood, he said sternly, "I'm going to need to see your ticket stub, Miss. And the others' too."

We had failed. There was no way from this point we could get back to the fifth or sixth car. We had to get off the train.

The determined look on Sarah's face told me all I needed to know. I saw her squeeze Dewey's hand, and he in turn squeezed back. Without a single word, I knew we would jump.

"Just a moment," I heard Sarah say to Mr. Corbitt as she pretended to look in her bag for the tickets.

The three of us stood in a knot near the opening. Dewey kept his eye out for a grassy place to jump. The train seemed to slow slightly as I saw a sign for the Bellvue Station. It was 7:09 A.M. I felt Dewey's strong hand slip into mine, and he whispered "On three."

The next moment I was flying through the air. We hit hard on soft ground, and before I could recover, Dewey was up and running in the same direction as the train. Mr. Corbitt watched with incredulity as Dewey made progress toward the speeding train. Four of the doomed wooden cars had passed us as we landed, but Dew was determined to catch up to the train and save his friend.

Sarah cried out, "Go, Jaxon!"

I bounded up and ran after Dewey, pumping my arms as hard as I could and stretching my long MacKenzie legs as far as they would go. I looked back at Sarah and saw her holding her arm, and as I turned my head to the front, I saw Dewey reach the last car before the caboose.

He reached up to grab hold of the car's railing with his right hand but he grasped a loose turn crank instead. As Dewey held on tightly, the crank came down hard on his left hand.

The next minute or so was in slow motion for me. I saw Dewey drop away from the train, holding his left hand in his right with a grimace of pain on his face. Blood spurted from his hand. I kept running past him.

My lungs burned as I took breath after breath. I could no longer feel my legs; they were a blur beneath me, and just when I felt I couldn't take another step, I saw Oliver standing at the rear of the car. His chocolate brown eyes were curious and smiling, and I strained toward him with everything I had in me.

He reached down to, no doubt, help me onto the train. I knew I had but this one chance, and I took the hand he offered and yanked him from the train. We fell with such force that we were a tangle of ebony and ivory arms and legs, and we rolled as one four-legged, four-armed crea-ture until we stopped next to a pebble-lined creek, which I would later learn was called Richland Creek. So close were we to the water that I was relieved we had come to a stop where we had, otherwise we would have been drenched.

We looked up as the tail end of the train made its way around Dutchman's bend, and instantly the sound of two

80-ton engines colliding made the ground shake and the waters next to us tremble. It was 7:15 A.M.

Without ceremony, Oliver Pack took my face in his mahogany hands, and kissed me on the forehead. "Thank you, Jaxon," he said with utmost sincerity. And just as I had known Sarah was my sister in this world, I knew then the mighty, handsome Oliver Pack would be my friend forever.

I sputtered something in reply, and then Oliver said, "How in the sam-hill did you get here?"

"We jumped aboard the train. It was your dream, Oliver. I realized on the platform at Bartlett that Dewey is my grandfather, and I knew then without a doubt that I came here to pull you from the train. You know, like in your dream? You pulled me from among the trees, and I pulled you out of the darkness."

"You mean you've been on this train all morning?"

"Yes," I replied breathlessly. "Sarah and Dewey are back a ways."

Then I remembered Dewey's injury.

"Dew's hurt," I said. "Let's go back down the track to find him and see what we can do to help."

Without brushing the debris from our clothing, we ran back about a quarter of a mile to where I had left Dewey. I breathlessly tried to explain our recent adventures to Oliver as we ran.

Sarah was already by Dewey's side, and had ripped some fabric from her clothes, which she was using to bind the tip of Dewey's finger. Her elbow was nearly black already from the bruise she had sustained when she hit the ground, and I could tell the spot was tender by the way she held her arm.

Dewey and Sarah glanced up when they heard us coming. From the amount of blood and the look of the binding, I was certain Dewey had cut off the tip of the pointer finger on his left hand.

"Are you alright?" we all seemed to ask at once.

Oliver and Dewey embraced like brothers, and I fell to my knees and wept. We had saved Oliver Pack.

I must admit my first impulse was to seek medical attention for Dewey's finger. I felt we should head back to the Bellvue Station. My mind raced as to how we would find help in the remote location in which we found ourselves. I had no thought of the passengers that were injured, dead and dying less than a mile from where we stood.

It was Oliver who insisted we find the wreck. He determined Dewey was not in shock, and our best chance of finding help for his finger was the one place where help was sure to be found before long, the crash site. Sarah carefully worked her arm to prove to Dewey and Oliver that no bones were broken in the fall.

The four of us walked somberly toward the crossing at White Bridge Road.

A photograph found at the crash site.

Chapter Twelve

Horror is the only word to describe what awaited us at the crash scene.

Through the black smoke blocking the view of the gently rolling hills, I couldn't tell where one train ended and the other began. It looked as if one train actually ran through the cars of the other train, like a telescope. Some cars hung off the embankment, many were on fire, and one car stood nearly on its end.

My mind raced as I looked for the wooden cars that until recently had held Oliver. These flimsy cars had turned to splinters, and there could not have been a living human among the carnage left by the six wooden coaches. Every one of the men I had passed as I searched in vain for Oliver, every single one, was dead nearly beyond recognition. The force of the crash, and the utter demolition of the wooden boxes in which they stood, splintered the men along with the wood. Every blade of grass, every tree trunk, every bush was spattered with blood. A small lake of blood had pooled around the splintered coaches. Body parts were scattered along with the debris. Ash from the burning cars drifted down from the heavens, and a blizzard of letters littered the ground. Somewhere in the mangled mess of metal was a mail car. The high pitched sound of despair rang out over the scene.

The four of us stood in place, silent. Death was tangible there in the air around us and in the smell of the burning coaches.

We were startled from our frozen positions by wails of agony that seemed to come from every direction.

"What should we do?" I asked Oliver.

"We have to help them," he said.

Sarah and I exchanged fearful glances. "But what should we do?" I asked again, knowing none of us knew where to begin.

Sarah said, "I think we should pray."

With the devastation around us, a moment of prayer was exactly what was needed. We held each other's hands and bowed our heads.

"Dear Heavenly Father," Dewey began. "Thank you for sparing our lives, and especially the life of our friend, Oliver. Help us to try to do what we can to assist those in need, even if all we can do is offer a prayer for their souls. In Jesus' name, amen."

I can't speak for the others, but I was buoyed by Dewey's simple prayer. I felt charged, energized for the endless hours before us. Where I had been queasy, I was strong. Where I felt helpless, I was assured any assistance I could give was a blessing. I can't say I've ever had a profound religious experience in my life, but at the tender age of twelve, our prayer prepared me for a day that would rival the worst than any war-seasoned veteran would endure.

The truth was, we were barely teenagers. Other first responders to the crash site sent their young children back home, sheltering them from the carnage. We should never have seen what we saw that day. It marked us. I'm sure of that. It wasn't until later I realized each of us never let the other three out of his or her sight all day. For all the terror that greeted us, we found comfort in knowing the four of us were together.

The living were so interspersed among the dead, that more than once I saw Oliver move several dead bodies before he could determine where the cries of the living originated. More often than not they were wails of those trapped beneath the train car, destined to die, and crying out in agony. A man whose hand was trapped beneath a piece of steel begged Oliver to cut off his hand so he could be freed.

Another man was pinned from the legs down beneath the upended rail car. His cries still echo in my mind. Had anyone been able to free him, he would have surely bled to death. Sarah prayed with him until he lost consciousness. He had a wife and three sons back in Memphis. They wouldn't learn of his death for nearly a week.

Oliver searched all day for George Scott among the living and the dead. He was nowhere to be found. To this day, I still have no idea what happened to him.

With the injury to his finger, Dewey couldn't move wood and metal the way Oliver could, so he helped stack the bodies onto horse-drawn carriages brought in from nearby farms to transport the dead to a series of morgues and make-shift morgues. There were times that awful day when strangers and volunteers mistook him with his blood drenched clothes for one of the seriously injured, and insisted that be seen by medical personnel.

Sarah and I helped the less seriously injured and directed them to volunteers who took down their names and addresses or home towns.

We needed to get word to the Hales and MacKenzies. Dewey wanted alert them as to where we were since our horse and buggy were still tied up to the tree by the Bartlett train station. They would no doubt be concerned as to the whereabouts of the four of us, and if the news of the train wreck had reached them, they deserved to know we were well. I asked a kindly woman to send a telegraph back to Bartlett to inform our families of where we were and that we were safe. I hoped Sarah's father could soften the news for Mrs. Hale. She, no doubt, would be furious. Oliver's mother also would need to be informed.

A feeble whisper for help caught our attention, and Sarah and I knelt down beside a woman whose unnatural position told us her lower half was crushed. Her clothing and her face were charred on one side. Someone had moved her from the wreckage and determined she was beyond saving. She had been laid out on the cool grass to die. The aquamarine ribbon in the woman's hair first drew my attention. With great sadness we recognized her peaceful expression as that of Bessie Dunn, the sweet-natured young widow who shared her stationery with us on the train. She could not have recognized us. Her eyes were glassy. Maybe she could already see the Divine.

"Mrs. Dunn," Sarah began.

"Take it," she painfully whispered around shallow gasps of air.

And with her last breath, she pressed her cherished ring into Sarah's hand for the last time.

As dusk began to fall, Sarah noticed a boy about our age looking over the destruction from White Bridge. He waved at us and motioned for us to join him. He held up a canteen of water and indicated we could drink from it. By that time, we would have done just about anything for a sip of water. Wearily we made our way up to drink and ask him if he knew of somewhere we could stay for the night.

His name was Frank Fletcher, and he had been one of the boys shooed away by his father when the enormity of the tragedy was first discovered. Frank spent his day bringing water to the bridge and offering it to volunteers. His father had instructed him not to venture past White Bridge until the wreck was cleared, and Frank was obliged to obey.

Frank was a slight boy with copper colored hair and a spattering of freckles across his nose. He wore round spectacles and often lifted them onto his forehead to squint into the distance as he looked at the wreckage below. He stammered slightly when he spoke, but we understood him perfectly and chose to wait patiently until Frank's mind and mouth could agree on a word pleasing to them both.

Frank's father was, like us, one of the first responders to the accident. Once summoned by his tirelessly waving and shouting son, Mr. Fletcher was agreeable to having us rest our weary heads at his house that night.

Mr. Fletcher and Oliver had worked together with the surviving train crew to raise the express car, heavy as it was, to try to free thirty trapped passengers. All but one were dead.

Mr. Fletcher and the rest of us shared our grim recollections of the day's gruesome discoveries as we trudged into the night to end the nightmare that was July 9, 1918. Most incredibly, Mr. Corbitt was found among the dead and taken to the morgue on the first load of the day. Dewey probably lifted him onto the wagon with the other bodies. Just as the mortician was preparing to embalm him, Mr. Corbitt moved. Unbelievably, he was alive. He was probably closest in proximity of all the passengers and crew to the six doomed wooden cars, and he lived. Someone said he would lose a leg, but as Oliver commented, "Better than losin' his life."

Although I could tell Mrs. Fletcher wasn't keen on having a colored boy sleep in her home, she took the greatest care of us that night, as though we were her own family. She cleaned and dressed Dewey's finger and gave us clean clothes to wear. We washed the dried blood from our faces and arms at the pump out back, scrubbing hard to remove the memory of it, but to no avail.

Before we dropped off to sleep, she laid her hand on each of our foreheads and sweetly said, "No eyes should ever have to see what you children saw today. There are no words I can speak to take it all away, but I promise I will pray for each one of you. If it be God's will, I pray you find peace tonight and always."

I clung to those words. I still do.

Chapter Thirteen

I didn't sleep much that night. My mind was restless. Sarah's curls reached across the cushion we shared as a pillow and tickled my face. My arms and legs ached from the strenuous day that lay behind me. There was a distant humming in my ears.

Sarah's hand rested next to her peaceful face, and in the dim light I could see Bessie Dunn's diamond ring on the third finger of Sarah's left hand. It was silver or white gold with a good sized diamond in the center and two smaller diamonds on either side. It was a little loose on Sarah's long, thin fingers, and it fell to one side. In her sleep, Sarah unconsciously worried it back into place.

Mrs. Fletcher had made up a bed for Sarah and me on the screened porch, the July heat had moved into the main part of the house, and I was thankful we had a cross breeze, even though the moving air was warm and thick with humidity. Dewey and Oliver slept in the cramped larder behind the kitchen where it smelled of Tennessee dirt and new potatoes.

A creak on the floorboards told me someone was coming to pay a visit, but although the moon shone through to the screen door, I could not see who it was. I sat up as the door opened.

Oliver made his way over to me without a sound, and the moonlight shone on the two streaks of tears that ran down his face. He reached down and pulled me to my feet, putting his finger to his lips in a gesture of silence.

I stood looking into those usually mirthful eyes that were now clouded with sorrow. He interlocked his fingers with mine. His hands were cool in the summer night. There were unspoken words on his lips, but he couldn't make them come. I knew the feeling. I had spent most of my life that way. His tears spoke for him.

Oliver grasped me in a hug that will go down in the history books as the best hug ever given. He lifted me off my feet and twirled me around in a circle. I imagined the soldiers as they returned home from war. This was the hug their battle-injured older brothers gave them upon first sight. It was the apex of filial love.

"Come with me," he whispered.

I followed him into the Fletcher's house, and he led me into the tiny parlor at the front of the house. I was nervous. I wasn't sure how the Fletchers would react to finding Oliver and me standing among their finest pieces of furniture.

"Let's go back out on the porch," I whispered.

"No, Jaxon. I think you need to see this." And with that said, Oliver pointed to a picture over Mrs. Fletcher's fireplace.

I was stunned.

It was an oil painting of a room with a bay window in the morning light. The pastels of the new dawn outside the painted window matched the fabric of Mrs. Fletcher's loveseat behind me. The painted sheer lace curtains were familiar to me, as was the dark green carpet. The artist had captured each fiber of the carpet, and I knew what it felt like to touch it because I had touched it many times. I stood transfixed by a perfect painting of my grandparents' parlor.

A creak of the floorboard announced someone was approaching. We guiltily turned, only to see Dewey eyeing us suspiciously.

"What are you doing in here?" he asked.

"It's the painting." I tried to explain. I couldn't take my eyes from the growing light in the familiar room.

"Go back to bed. Oliver, you're going to get us all thrown out of here, sneaking around with a white girl in the middle of the night. The Fletcher's were nervous enough just taking us in."

"It's not like that, Dew." Oliver was hurt.

"It'll look like it to them." Dewey gestured toward the staircase and the sleeping Fletchers.

"Dewey," I said. He turned to me and searched my face, almost pleadingly. "Grandpa. This is where we live."

I reached for his hand and felt the bandage on his finger. "That door," I continued pointing to a door in the painting, "leads to the kitchen. And that little door over there is a closet under the stair where you keep games and puzzles for me. That willow tree, you see it just out the window there, we planted it together the first day I moved in with you. Look how tall it is now. It looked like a twig with leaves on it when we planted it. I never thought it would grow. Now we hang bird feeders in it for Grandma so she can sit in her chair there, right there, and watch the little yellow finches flit back and forth for the sunflower seeds we grow in our garden out back.

"And that little square grate over there. Do you see it? That's where the heat comes up in the winter. The metal gets so hot I can only stand there for a few seconds, but I love to come down in my bare feet and nightgown and the air flows up and fills my nightgown with warmth. Sometimes I try to straddle the grate so I can stand there longer without burning the pads of my feet. You always tell me I'm going to catch a cold without my robe and slippers, but I never wear them, and you never scold me for it.

"And the little lopsided clay vase on the windowsill. See it? I made it when I was seven. And the roses inside it? We grow them for Grandma. And do you see the tiny little crack in the window next to the vase? That happened when a big truck spun its tires in the snow and threw a rock at our window. We still haven't fixed that crack."

It was time for me to go home. We all knew it. This was my chance to go back to where I belonged. There was a second, fleeting and brief, when I thought of returning to the porch and going back to sleep — of living this life with these friends. Of giving up the opportunity to go home. But something greater still yearned for home, and so, without speaking a word of my reservations about leaving, I said, "Let's awaken Sarah."

She startled when we nudged her to find three pairs of eyes on her. "What's wrong?" were the first words she uttered.

Dewey replied, "It's time for Jaxon to go home."

"But how?" Sarah muttered as she stepped further into wakefulness.

I said, "There's a painting in the parlor over the fireplace. It's my way home."

aying goodbye to Oliver and Sarah was harder than I expected. I knew I'd see Dewey, old-wrinkled-bald Dewey, at home, and it wouldn't be the same as young, strong, life-ahead-of-him Dewey. But somehow knowing he would be there was a comfort.

I wasn't so sure I'd see Sarah or Oliver again.

First I approached Oliver. I took his handsome face in both of my hands and put one of my thumbs over each dimple that I had grown to love. He looked down at me and smiled into my eyes while tears rolled down his face. Our exchange reminded me of a rainbow, an unspoken promise. I would love Oliver Pack every day of my life.

Dewey was next and our hug was quick. He wasn't an overly sentimental kind of guy, and our goodbye was akin to pulling off a band-aid: fast and painful.

I turned to Sarah. She was sobbing silently, her shoulders shaking. Stray curls stuck to the tears on her face. With one finger, I pushed them back behind her ear with the rest of her unruly mane.

"Your hand brought me here," I said. "Will you help me find my way home?"

She nodded and we embraced. As we pulled apart, I wiped the tears from her face with my thumbs. The boys each stood with their arms straight down in front of them and their fingers laced together to give me a boost over the fireplace and into the painting. Sarah steadied me as I stepped into their hands. I felt the pressure of her hand on my back as I reached out to touch the painting.

I grasped the bottom of the frame and leaned forward.

s I felt Sarah's reassuring hand pushing me from behind, through the painting, I sensed a rush of lightning through my arm as another hand pulled me back into the present. The long slender fingers were softer than silk, and on the third finger of the left hand was a ring that fell to the side. I felt her quickly worry it with her thumb.

The first sensation I experienced was the rushing of wind against my skin. I could not decide if I was floating or standing still or flying. I felt weightless, only anchored by the soft hand holding fast to mine.

The wind moved around me but produced no noise. I noticed a complete absence of sound. The comforting words of my friends were gone. The familiar sounds of the southern summer had been absorbed in silence.

I realize my eyes were closed. I opened them. Swirling around me in a sea of color were images from my home, pieces of furniture, flashes of light. I saw the world before me; I was part of it, merging with life and gravity.

Even though I should have been scared, I felt calm. I looked into the eyes of the old woman in front of me.

Suddenly I fell into the ample arms of my dear grandmother. A smile lit up her face, and I noticed the hint of a dimple in her cheek. The shock of recognition hit me.

Before I realized it, tears of joy pricked at my eyelids, and I croaked out her name. "Sarah."

Chapter Fourteen

I'd like to tell you that I regained my speech from the time I re-emerged into my own world, but I can't. My speech is still severely limited. It always will be. I still hum when I am upset, and rock and hum when I am really, really upset.

What I *can* tell you is that my grandparents, Sarah and Dewey, their dear friend Oliver Pack, and his incredibly handsome grandson Michael are teaching me sign language, and I am learning to communicate using a computer.

I keep no more secrets. Everyone, including my mother, knows I can read, and they keep me well supplied with books. Mother is amazed at the growth I've shown over recent weeks, and she is less vocal with my grandparents regarding the group home. She still keeps her distance from me, though. I know I am the spitting image of my dad, and his name was Jackson MacKenzie, not so unlike mine. It is hard for Mother to live without him, and I've seen the kind of pain she suffers in the eyes of my dear grandparents when they speak of their son.

The first time I saw Oliver after returning home, I was shocked. Life had been hard on him. He stoops when he walks, and his hands and face, once so smooth and irresistible, are now weathered with age. The sparkle in his chocolate brown eyes remains untouched, though, by his many years. He tells me he married young, a Miss Louetta Jean Browning, and he and Lucy, as he calls her, had five daughters and one son. Lucy died the year I was born, and the girls take turns looking in on Oliver to make sure he's eating well and keeping the house clean. His son, Ellison, lives one town over and comes to visit on Sundays. He brings Oliver's grandson, Michael, with him.

Even though my grandparents and Oliver were written up in the Bartlett city newspaper the day after the crash, and they became local celebrities for a time, my great grandmother, Mrs. Hale, sent Sarah away that fall to school in Huntington, West Virginia, where Sarah lived with her maternal aunt, away from the distractions of the MacKenzie farm. Sarah played basketball in honest-to-goodness bloomers for Huntington High's first girl's basketball team. I have a picture to prove it. Grandma said it was scandalous for the girls to have cut their hair and played at a sport. Mrs. Hale was not amused, I'm sure.

Dewey moved to Huntington during Sarah's first year at Marshall College there. He sold cemetery plots before taking a job at the post office, where he would work until he retired. Mrs. Hale finally saw fit to accept him as a son when he and Sarah took her in to live with them as her health failed. Yet, she never quit calling him "that MacKenzie boy."

Olivia MacKenzie Pack

Grandma and me on the happiest day of my life, my wedding day.

Olivia MacKenzie Pack

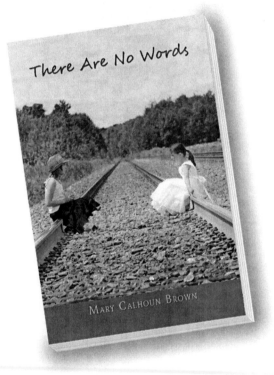

There Are No Words
Readers' Guide

In *There Are No Words* Mary Calhoun Brown tells the story of a twelve-year-old girl, Jaxon, being raised by her grandparents in the present day. Jaxon faces unique challenges in her life, yet finds herself in the position of being able to save her beloved grandfather's best friend, Oliver Pack. Through the friendship of Oliver, Sara, and Dewey, Jaxon accomplishes more than some people might have thought possible, and she does it by going back in time.

Though this book is a work of fiction, the author based the story on a real-life event, a train wreck in Tennesse in 1918. Therefore, *There Are No Words* is considered *historical fiction*. The author has imagined people and events and how they may have behaved during an historical event.

There are many instances in literature where characters embark on what is known as a *hero's quest.* This is when the main character is faced with a task that may seem impossible for him (or her) to undertake. Yet in meeting the challenge, he becomes the person he was meant to be and fulfills his destiny. In a similar way, Mary Calhoun Brown has given Jaxon a task that seems impossible: the task of going back in time and changing history. As Jaxon meets this challenge, we are able to see beyond her limitations and understand more about her as a person with thoughts and feelings.

Think about the questions on the following pages and consider what you might learn from Jaxon's experiences that could either help you face challenges in your own life, or help you to understand people who seem very different from yourself.

1.   In the opening of the book, Jaxon describes the carpet in some detail. To what other concepts from the book could the author be alluding?

2.   a. Compare and contrast Jaxon's mother with Mrs. Hale, Sarah's mother.

        b. Compare Jaxon's mother with Jaxon's grandparents.

3.   How does Jaxon's description of the rain show you her sensitivity?

4.   What do the four pieces of the old newspaper represent?

5.   a. How can you tell Jaxon is different from other children?

        b. Can you tell she is autistic? How?

6.   How do Jaxon, Grandma, and Grandpa's favorite colors of roses reflect their personalities?

7.   The author indicates a "locked gate" in the garden with its "hinges rusted shut long ago." To what could she be alluding?

8.   What does Jaxon's description of the first appearance of Oliver tell us about her?

9.   Compare and contrast race relations in 1918 to the way Jaxon is treated in the present.

10. Mrs. Hale "saved her kindnesses for those of her limited acquaintance, rather than those in her immediate family and her neighborhood."

    a. Do you know anyone like this?

    b. Why would Sarah's mother behave in this way?

11. What do Jaxon's scuffed shoes represent?

12. Compare and contrast Oliver Pack and George Scott.

13. When did you first see Dewey begin to transform into Grandpa?

14. Who is the hero in this book?

15. How do you think Dewey feels about the glimpse Jaxon gives him of his future?

16. If you were Jaxon, would you stay in 1918 or go home?

17. a. What does the photo of the little girl on page 115 suggest about the end of the story?

    b. Why do you think the author chose to end her book with it?

    c. What story does the little girl's name tell?

Mary Calhoun Brown

Photograph by Janet Wise McCormick

About the Author

Mary Calhoun Brown tells stories about things that matter, weaving colorful and sensitive characters into history for a generation that prefers to be entertained rather than educated.

Brown has spent most of her professional career writing and editing non-fiction. She wrote extensively for the West Virginia Chamber of Commerce before moving on to help create the Partnership for Financial Education.

Brown is an advocate for children and adults with autism. She also partners with educators to create curriculum guides for her novels so teachers and home-school parents can meet state requirements while making the most of classroom and planning time.

Mary Calhoun Brown lives in beautiful Huntington, West Virginia, with her husband Cam and three sons: William, Harrison, and Dewey.

Appendix

Recommended Websites

Mary Calhoun Brown recommends the following websites for more information. Permission to print this list has been granted by Tony Attwood (www.tonyattwood.com.au). A second list with additional U.S.-based websites follows on page 125.

www.ahaNY.org — AHA Association is a New York organization providing support and information for families, individuals, and professionals affected by Asperger's Syndrome (AS), High Functioning (H/F) Autism, Pervasive Developmental Disorders (PDD) and related conditions.

www.angelfire.com/amiga/aut — This is the website of Kevin, who was diagnosed in May 2000 with Asperger's Syndrome.

www.aspennj.org — ASPEN® Asperger Syndrome Education Network Inc. ASPEN® is a regionally based non-profit organization based in New Jersey with 12 local chapters providing support and information to families and individuals with AS, PDD-NOS (not otherwise specified), HFA, and related disorders.

www.aspergeradults.ca — Maintained by a middle-aged woman, a professional writer, with Asperger's Syndrome; she also writes for www.suite101.com/welcome.cfm/adult_aspergers

http://www.aspergernauts.co.uk — Aspergernauts — An animated Site.

www.aspergers.co.nz — This website, maintained by Jen Birch, seeks to give basic information on Autistic Spectrum Disorder, with an emphasis on the higher-functioning types of Asperger's Syndrome and High-Functioning Autism.

www.asperger-training.com — Sarah Hendrickx plus two colleagues with AS provide training to organizations and 1:1 support to individuals and couples where one or both partners has AS. Co-author (with AS partner, Keith) of *Asperger Syndrome: A Love Story* and other AS titles. UK-based.

www.aspie.com – The website of Liane Holliday-Willey, Ed.D.

www.autismnz.org.nz — Autism New Zealand Inc.

www.autismandcomputing.org.uk — Autism and computing is a non-profit group that hosts helpful articles for people with Asperger's syndrome on its website, including Marc Segars' "Survival Guide for people with Asperger-Syndrome."

www.autismawarenesscentre.com — Resource and educational organization that hosts workshops in Canada and overseas. Books available online.

www.autismforum.net — Personal experiences with Asperger's syndrome. Chat room and forum available.

www.autismhangout.com — Autism Hangout is an online discussion forum that reports news, complies facts and community-submitted personal experiences and invites ongoing discussion to discover insights on how best to deal with the daily challenges of autism.

www.colour-se7en.co.uk — A point of reference on the World Wide Web for information on the subject of Asperger's Syndrome and other Autistic Spectrum-related disorders.

www.freewebs.com/assupportgroup — Leicestershire, UK is the home of this young teenager with Asperger's syndrome.

www.geocities.com/a_u_t_a_p/ — South Australian woman with AS working with people with ASDs. Looking at different perspectives presented on ASDs from around the world. Also researching Gender Identity in individuals with AS.

www.geocities.com/environmental1st2003/Main1.html — Tom is an Aspie.

health.groups.yahoo.com/group/AspieFriendFinder — Aspie Friend Finder — Online Group for Aspie Teens and Tweens.

health.groups.yahoo.com/group/FAMSecretShield/ — Message board for people with AS & HFA who have been bullied at home/work/school/etc.

health.groups.yahoo.com/group/FAMSecretSociety/ — Message board for people with AS & HFA.

www.isn.net/~jypsy — Oops...Wrong Planet Syndrome. This provides a personal and informative perspective on Asperger's Syndrome.

www.people.freenet.de/anaid — Diana's Personal Asperger Page. Diana is from Germany and her site is in English and German.

www.thehelpgroup.org — The Help Group conducts 6 specialized day schools providing programs to 1100 students with special needs related to: autism, A/S, learning disabilities, mental retardation, abuse and emotional problems.

www.treg.org.uk — The Rightway Education Group aims to find the right way to support families and individuals with Asperger's and HFA while educating the community by raising awareness. UK-based.

www.webspawner.com/users/asperger — George Handley's webpage. George has Asperger's Syndrome and writes about himself and how he copes with life.

welkowitz.typepad.com — Asperger's Podcast. Weekly online radio program on A/S suitable for download to MP3 players.

www.wrongplanet.net — Website inspired by two friends with Asperger's syndrome.

www-users.cs.york.ac.uk/~alistair/survival/ or

www.asperger-marriage.info/survguide/contents.html — This link enables you to access and download Marc Segar's book *Coping: A Survival Guide for People with Asperger's Syndrome.*

Publisher's Recommended U.S. Websites:

American Academy of Pediatrics: Autistic disorder, Asperger syndrome, pervasive developmental disorder NOS – www.aap.org/healthtopics/Autism.cfm

Autism Fact Sheet from the National Institute of Neurological Disorders and Stroke: www.ninds.nih.gov/disorders/autism/detail_autism.htm

Autism Information Center (US Dept. of Health & Human Services/CDC): www.cdc.gov/ncbddd/autism

Autism Research Institute: www.autism.com – "The Autism Research Institute (ARI), a non-profit organization, was established in 1967. For more than 40 years, ARI has devoted its work to conducting research, and to disseminating the results of research, on the triggers of autism and on methods of diagnosing and treating autism. We provide research-based information to parents and professionals around the world." ARI's Call Center — English: 1-866-366-3361 Español: 877-644-1184 ext. 5

Autism Resources Site: www.autism-resources.com – Maintained by John Wobus.

Autism Science Foundation: www.autismsciencefoundation.org – "The Autism Science Foundation's mission is to support autism research by providing funding and other assistance to scientists and organizations conducting, facilitating, publicizing and disseminating autism research. The organization also provides information about autism to the general public and serves to increase awareness of autism spectrum disorders and the needs of individuals and families affected by autism. Our organization adheres to rigorous scientific standards and values. We believe that outstanding research is the greatest gift we can offer our families."

Autism Society of America: www.autism-society.org – The primary mission of ASAF is to raise and allocate funds to address the many unanswered questions about autism.

Autism Speaks: www.autismspeaks.org – "Autism Speaks was founded in February 2005 by Bob and Suzanne Wright, grandparents of a child with autism. Since then, Autism Speaks has grown into the largest autism science and advocacy organization in the US, dedicated to funding research into the causes, prevention, treatments and a cure for autism; increasing awareness of autism spectrum disorders; and advocating for the needs of individuals with autism and their families.."

Easter Seals and Autism: autismblog.easterseals.com

First Signs: www.firstsigns.org – "First Signs is dedicated to educating parents and professionals about the early warning signs of autism and related disorders."

My Sad Is All Gone: www.luckypress.com – This is the first published book by a Canadian parent of a child with autism, Thelma Wheatley. It is also available on Amazon.com and is published by Lucky Press, LLC, publisher of *There Are No Words.*

The National Autism Society: www.autism.org.uk (UK-based)

Online Asperger Syndrome Information and Support (OASIS): www.aspergersyndrome.org/

Pervasive Developmental Disorders: The National Institute of Mental Health – www.nimh.nih.gov/health/publications/autism/complete-index.shtml

Special Needs Camps: http://www.campresource.com/summer-camps/special-needs-camps.cfm/aspergers-camps

What's Unique about Asperger's Disorder?: www.autism-society.org/site/PageServer?pagename=life_aspergers

For more information on the Great Train Wreck of 1918, please see the following:

www.dutchmanscurve.com

**A free curriculum guide is available
to teachers upon request.
Go to www.marycalhounbrown.com
for more information.**

Lucky Press, LLC is a traditional, independent publishing company located in the beautiful Appalachian foothills of Athens, Ohio. Founded in 1999, it became an LLC and published its first title in 2000. From its original aim to publish books about "characters, real or imagined, who overcome adversity or experience adventure," Lucky Press has given exposure to worthwhile authors who might have been overlooked by larger houses, and expanded into the categories of health, pets, and special needs. Write to Lucky Press at PO Box 754, Athens, OH 45701-0754 or send an email to books@ luckypress.com.

Books for Kids, Teens, and Young Adults from Lucky Press, LLC

The Aviator's Apprentice
Turner's Flight
Turner's Defense
(www.luckypress.com/chrisdavey.html)

Guardian Spirit
(www.luckypress.com/sarahmartinbyrd.html)

The Life and Times of Mister
(www.luckypress.com/jrm.html)

Max and Menna
(www.luckypress.com/shaunakelley.html)

There Are No Words
(www.luckypress.com/marycalhounbrown.html)

They Called Me Beautiful:
A Dog's Search for Love and the Family that Rescued Him
(www.luckypress.com/janicephelpswilliams.html)

Learn about these titles and more at www.LuckyPress.com.

LaVergne, TN USA
22 October 2010
201880LV00005B/1/P